TEQUILA SHOOTERS

Slocum drew, the others reaching for their guns just a
beat behind him. Toby was supposed to be the fastest,
and a left-hand draw was tricky, so Slocum shot him
first. Then he put one dead center into Sim Treece, and
another into Brick. The shots came so fast, they sounded
like one continuous blast. The gun bucked in Slocum's
hand, spitting fire, smoke, thunder, and lead.

Toby whirled, spinning, falling. Sim Treece's guns
had both cleared the holster when he was tagged. He
went over backward, like a tin target in a shooting gallery. Dying, he reflexively jerked the triggers, shooting
harmlessly into the sky.

Slocum felt the breeze of Brick's bullet whiz past his
head. His shot had taken Brick in the right side of the
chest. He'd been aiming for the heart, but Brick had
been turning and the shot had missed.

The impact knocked Brick to his knees. He was shot
through the lung, but the gun was still in his hand. He
fired, missing Slocum but shattering the tequila bottle in
a spray of liquid and flying glass.

''Why, you son of a bitch!'' Slocum said, shooting
him dead . . .

DON'T MISS THESE
ALL-ACTION WESTERN SERIES
FROM THE BERKLEY PUBLISHING GROUP

THE GUNSMITH by J. R. Roberts
> Clint Adams was a legend among lawmen, outlaws, and ladies. They called him . . . the Gunsmith.

LONGARM by Tabor Evans
> The popular long-running series about U.S. Deputy Marshal Long—his life, his loves, his fight for justice.

SLOCUM by Jake Logan
> Today's longest-running action Western. John Slocum rides a deadly trail of hot blood and cold steel.

BUSHWHACKERS by B. J. Lanagan
> An action-packed series by the creators of Longarm! The rousing adventures of the most brutal gang of cutthroats ever assembled— Quantrill's Raiders.

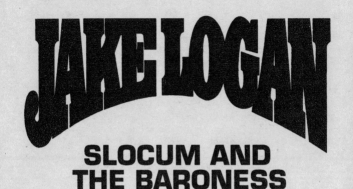

SLOCUM AND
THE BARONESS

JOVE BOOKS, NEW YORK

SLOCUM AND THE BARONESS

A Jove Book / published by arrangement with
the author

PRINTING HISTORY
Jove edition / January 1999

ISBN: 0-515-12436-2

A JOVE BOOK®
Jove Books are published by The Berkley Publishing Group, a member
of Penguin Putnam Inc.,
375 Hudson Street, New York, New York 10014.
JOVE and the "J" design are trademarks belonging to
Jove Publications, Inc.

PRINTED IN THE UNITED STATES OF AMERICA

10 9 8 7 6 5 4 3 2 1

SLOCUM AND
THE BARONESS

1

From where he sat, Slocum could pretty much see all of the town. It was a small town, this Los Palos, New Mexico, a handful of buildings grouped around a dusty crossroads in the middle of nowhere. But there was fresh springwater here, and that was enough for a settlement to grow up on the site. That had happened about two centuries earlier, when the Spanish conquistadors had first thrust northward out of their colony in Mexico City.

Now, it was modern times: 1889. The town hadn't changed much since its original founding. At the center of town, there was an open plaza, unpaved. At its center was a cistern, an aboveground circular stone basin. The walls were three feet high and two feet wide. The basin was eight feet across. It was fed by a spring, and there were catch-pools for the runoff.

Buildings lined the edge of the plaza, mostly flat-roofed one-story whitewashed adobe cubes. They had square holes for the windows and oblong holes for the doorways. In the noonday sun of this late spring day, the white walls were glaring and the holes were inky black. The basin looked like it was filled with molten metal.

On the west side of the plaza stood a two-story courthouse built and run by the Anglos, the most recent arrivals to dominate these parts. Nearby were some wooden frame buildings, hotels, saloons, a general store, and similar establishments. No trees grew on this sunbaked flat, and the timber for the buildings had had to be freighted in.

Most of the town's population of a few hundred souls were of Spanish descent, with a relative handful of whites. The newcomers had a lion's share of what trade and political power there was to be had. If they got in trouble, they could call on the U.S. cavalry. If they were lucky, the cavalry might even someday show up, though too late to be of any use.

Still, it was a peaceful town, if only because there wasn't much of anything worth killing over, no gold or silver mines, no real cattle wealth. A few years earlier, there had been a real dustup in Lincoln County, involving the likes of Billy the Kid and Pat Garrett, but that had been far away, in a distant part of the territory. It had pulled in a lot of bad hombres, more than a few of whom were still around.

It was especially peaceful now, on a weekday noon, when nobody went out under the sun who didn't have to. The plaza was nearly deserted, except for a few passersby on various routine errands, and they got out of the sun as soon as they could.

On the north side of the plaza was a cantina, a rectangular box whose long sides ran east-west. It had white stucco walls, with the ends of roof beams sticking out at the top. On the east side of the building, there was a patio with a bare dirt floor, roofed over by a wood-frame sunshade canopy. The frame was made of rows of eight-foot-tall vertical poles, supporting a flat wooden grid. The grid was crisscrossed with dozens of thin poles, forming a lattice that screened out most of the sun.

Under the canopy it was cool and shady, with dusty sunbeams slanting through it at odd angles. There was a trestle table, and a couple of chairs made out of logs.

Slocum sat in one of the chairs, feet up on the table, facing the plaza. A low-crowned wide-brimmed hat was pulled down low in front. He wore a blue denim shirt with the sleeves rolled up, a red engineer's bandanna knotted around his neck, a black leather vest with silver conchos, gray-brown jeans, and boots. He was deep-tanned, sunburnished, the hairs on his brawny forearms like little copper wires. He wore a holstered Colt on his right hip. The well-worn gun belt was like old saddle leather. The gun was latent with deadly power. So was he.

A knife was stuck into the wooden tabletop in front of him, an eighteen-inch-long knife with elk-horn handles and a foot-long razor-sharp blade. It was his knife. It looked like a small sword. Nearby was a thick glass tumbler, a plate with a couple of limes and a small mound of rough-grained salt, and a bottle of tequila.

A bare dirt strip stood between the patio and the cantina. The square-cut deep-set windows in the structure showed that the adobe walls were about a foot thick. The inside was filled with warm brown shadows. From time to time, a figure flitted past the windows, the cook or one of the servers. Within, there were the sounds of activity in the kitchen, rustlings and scrapings.

There was a pleasing scent of coffee, cornmeal, chili powder, and woodsmoke from a cooking fire, mingled with the flinty smell of alkali dust. Behind the back of the building, irrigation troughs watered a small vegetable garden.

Even in the shade it was hot, but it was a good dry heat that warmed the bones. Slocum soaked it up. He was on the way toward starting to soak up a fair amount of tequila too.

He splashed a nice-sized slug of the cactus juice into the glass, pulled the knife out of the tabletop, and cut a lime into quarters. He wiped the blade clean on his pants, then stuck it into a table plank, so that it stood upright, not far from his hand.

He put a pinch of salt on the web of his hand, between thumb and forefinger. He licked the salt, gulped the tequila, and bit into a slice of lime.

The tequila bit back, the way he liked it. He shuddered, saying "Whew!"

He broke out into a fresh sweat, droplets glimmering like tiny seed crystals on his sun-bronzed face. Some got into his eyes, stinging. He wiped them with the back of his hand. His eyes were blue-gray, standing out against his dark burnished skin.

The sky was bright blue, with a fierce yellow-white sun blazing at the zenith. The sky was bare of both clouds and birds. The air was still, except in the west.

There was a lot of commotion in the west, on the road outside town. There was a cloud of dust rising somewhere in the middle distance. It was next to impossible to cross the dry, gritty landscape without raising a telltale track of dust.

West of town, the ground was flat tableland for fifty miles, before fetching up against the east face of the rugged Sangre de Cristo mountain range. North, south, and east, Los Palos was surrounded by open emptiness.

The dust cloud was closer now. It was more of a pillar than a cloud, a thick vertical chalk stripe notching the middle of the horizon.

Most travelers in these parts moved during the morning or in the late afternoon, when the sun was lower. Whoever was approaching must have a good reason to go riding in the noonday heat.

They were in a hurry too, judging by the size of the cloud they were raising.

Further west, there was a second line of dust in the sky. Maybe somebody was getting chased.

The town was far from any railroad lines. Stagecoaches came through once or twice a week, but there were none scheduled for today, as far as Slocum knew. He'd been in town for a few days, waiting, long enough to have picked up the local routine.

There was time for another tequila before the source of the dust had resolved itself into three riders. They slowed as they rode into town, to the west side of the plaza. They got down off their horses. Three men. It was too far away to make out much more than that.

One held the reins of the horses, while the others looked around. They were looking for something, or somebody. There weren't many townsfolk out and around, but those who were were approached by the newcomers, who seemed to be asking a lot of questions.

After a minute or two, the trio regrouped. They stood facing the cantina from across the plaza. They put their heads together. One of them pointed at the cantina. They all nodded.

They broke apart, looking back the way they had come. The dust they had kicked up had settled, but the second cloud, the one behind them, still hung in the air, a feathery plume. It was closer to town, but not so close that its source could be made out.

The three climbed on their horses, pointed them at the cantina, and started across the plaza at a quick walk.

Slocum got up, crossing to the building. His gait was loose, unhurried. Plenty loose, thanks to the tequila. But still tight enough.

He stuck his head through the window, into the cantina. There was a square-shaped common room with a couple of tables and some chairs, and a long counter that served as a bar at the opposite end of the space. To one side of the bar, an open doorway led back into the kitchen at the rear of the building.

The chairs were stacked on top of the tables, except for one table off by itself in a corner. The owner sat there, eating his lunch. He was a heavyset man, with thinning black hair and a thick handlebar mustache. His plate was heaped high, and he was digging into it with gusto.

He looked up, seeing Slocum. He froze, holding his fork in midair, his mouth open.

Slocum said, "Better lay low and keep your head down for a couple of minutes."

The owner's eyes bulged. He pushed back from the table and stood up, not asking questions. He knew trouble when he saw it.

His fat wife came out of the kitchen, standing in the doorway to see what it was all about. He yelled at her to get moving and round up the others. For a heavy woman, she could move pretty fast. The owner moved fast too, closing the wooden window shutters.

Out the back door came the owner's family: two unattractive daughters, the missus, and lastly, the owner himself. He closed the door behind him, not locking it, then followed the others behind the back of the building, around the corner, and away.

Slocum slipped the leather thong loop at the top of his gun, freeing it for the draw. He went back to the patio, to the table, but didn't sit down. He stood waiting, arms hanging loose at his sides, right shoulder dipped slightly lower than the left. He looked as if he didn't have a care in the world.

The riders came on three abreast, altering their course slightly when they saw Slocum, angling toward him. They moved at a nice easy pace, for which the horses seemed grateful. The animals had been ridden hard, the sweat foaming up into a lather. Their heads drooped as they plodded onward.

The trio reined in their horses a few paces short of the edge of the patio. They swung down from the saddle, three hard-bitten characters, powdered with road dust.

The one in the middle said, "Slocum?"

"Who wants to know?" Slocum said.

The three exchanged side glances. The one who had spoken said, "The Treece brothers." He said it as if it was supposed to mean something.

"I'm Sim Treece, and these are my brothers, Brick and Toby," he said.

Sim Treece, the eldest, was gangling and storklike, with a long, straggly graying goatee. He wore a dark suit and pants, a fancy brocaded vest, and two guns.

On his right was Brick, younger but still middle-aged, a big sloppy man with ginger-colored hair and an angry red face with a lot of jaw and not much forehead. His meaty hand hovered heavily over his holstered gun.

Toby, the youngest, was lean and athletic, his good looks spoiled by cold eyes and a sneering mouth. He was something of a dude, with a fancy silver-and-turquoise hatband, a fringed buckskin shirt, and fancy silver stirrups with oversized star rowels. He was a left-handed draw.

Brick Treece thrust his jaw forward belligerently, saying, "Maybe you heard of us, huh?"

"No," Slocum said.

Brick snorted, taking a step forward. Sim raised a hand to restrain him. His other hand held his horse's reins.

"You're hearing about us now," Toby said.

"I was just joshing. I've heard of you," Slocum said.

"The way you say it, it doesn't sound like you heard anything nice," Sim Treece said, smiling.

"What do you want?"

"Get right to the point, don't you? That's good, I like

that. So I'll get to the point too. This town's not healthy for you, Slocum. Get out now, while you can.''

''I like it fine here.''

Toby said, ''We can fix that.''

Sim Treece glanced at the bottle of tequila. ''He's drunk.''

''Not hardly,'' Slocum said, his words thick. He swayed a little, as if he had trouble standing up straight.

''Pour his drunk ass on a horse and get him out of here before I lose my temper,'' Toby said.

''Why do you want me out? I've got no quarrel with you,'' Slocum said, speaking to Sim Treece, ignoring the others.

''If you had a quarrel with us, you'd be dead,'' Sim Treece said, still smiling. ''Nothing personal. That's why you get a chance to ride out with a whole skin.

''So, take your bottle and git.''

''Tell you what. Suppose you get back on your horses and ride out instead,'' Slocum said.

''Hell, Sim, he's just playing with you. He's just a damned drunk,'' Brick said.

''You like to play, huh, mister?'' Toby said, licking his lips, savoring the flavor of the coming kill.

''Who sent you?'' Slocum said.

Sim Treece stopped smiling. ''You ask too many questions.''

''Here's one more. Where do you want the bodies sent?''

He drew, the others reaching for their guns just a beat behind him. Toby was supposed to be the fastest, and a left-hand draw was tricky, so Slocum shot him first. Then he put one dead center into Sim Treece, and another into Brick. The shots came so fast, they sounded like one continuous blast. The gun bucked in Slocum's hand, spitting fire, smoke, thunder, and lead.

Toby whirled, spinning, falling. Sim Treece's guns had

both cleared the holster when he was tagged. He went over backward, like a tin target in a shooting gallery. Dying, he reflexively jerked the triggers, shooting harmlessly into the sky.

Slocum felt the breeze of Brick's bullet whizz past his head. His shot took Brick in the right side of the chest. He'd been aiming for the heart, but Brick had been turning and the shot had missed.

The impact knocked Brick to his knees. He was shot through the lung, but the gun was still in his hand. He fired, missing Slocum but shattering the tequila bottle in a spray of liquid and flying glass.

"Why, you son of a bitch!" Slocum said, shooting him dead.

The horses, spooked, reared up and ran away. They were tired and didn't run far.

Slocum surveyed the damage, sadly shaking his head.

"Ain't that a kick in the ass . . . plenty of limes and salt left, but no tequila!"

2

A cloud of gun smoke hung in the air. With barely a breath of a breeze to disturb it, it looked as if it had been painted in place.

Slocum reloaded, then went into the cantina. Inside, it was cooler and dim. He went behind the bar and got a bottle of tequila and another glass, leaving a coin in payment on the bar.

He went outside. The cloud of gun smoke was beginning to break up into long horizontal layers. Around the plaza, people were starting to stick their heads up to see what had happened. The more time passed without a fresh round of shooting, the more they began to show themselves. Nobody came over to investigate, though.

Nobody but the law, that is. Two figures came out of the jailhouse on the southwest side of the plaza and started across the open space. One was big and bullish, the one in the lead. The other was thin, reedy. It was Sheriff Dan Bigelow and his deputy, Virgil. Sunlight glinted off the badge pinned to Bigelow's chest. He was carrying a double-barreled shotgun under one arm.

Slocum had time for a drink before they reached the

cantina. By the time they drew near, the gun smoke had mostly broken up. Bigelow was stolid, unemotional. He carried the shotgun pointed downward. His deputy was more excited. He was jumpy, nervous. He had a gun in his hand.

Slocum took out his gun, pointing it in the deputy's general direction while the lawmen were still a stone's throw away.

"That deputy of yours looks a little shaky, Dan. Tell him to put away his gun before he hurts himself," Slocum said.

Bigelow glanced back at his deputy, a few paces behind him. He frowned, saying, "Dammit, Virgil, put that iron away."

Virgil was weedy, with pop eyes. "B-b-but, Sheriff, he killed three men!"

"He's all right. Now, do as you're told."

Virgil reluctantly holstered his gun. Bigelow said, "The next time I catch you with a drawn gun behind me, I'm gonna kick your butt."

Slocum put up his weapon. Virgil's eyes bulged wider as he stared at the dead men. Bigelow said, "You said you weren't going to make trouble in my town, Slocum."

"I didn't. They did," Slocum said, indicating the dead.

Bigelow nodded, satisfied. He was over fifty, heavyset, but not soft, with a craggy balding head and whiskery jowls. His gun belt was worn low over a big gut. Inside a nest of wrinkles, his eyes were long, narrow, and clear. Like many who wore the badge, he'd been on both sides of the law at various times. He knew Slocum from times past, and they got along well enough. They'd had a couple of drinks together since Slocum had first come to town a few days ago and found out that Bigelow was the local law.

"Who were they, Slocum?"

"The Treece brothers, Dan."

"Huh! What's their quarrel with you?"

Slocum shrugged. "Beats me."

"Sure," Bigelow said, openly skeptical.

"I ain't lying. They rode up and told me to get out of town."

"Just like that, huh?"

"Just like that."

"Could be," Bigelow said, noncommittal.

"A clear-cut case of self-defense," Slocum said.

"Could be. You search 'em?"

"I saved that for you."

"You and me could get along," Bigelow said. He turned to Virgil, saying, "Go get a doctor."

"What for? They're dead," Virgil said.

"Awright, then, get the undertaker. Just get."

"Yessir." Virgil hurried away, angling toward the west side of town.

"Weaselly-looking dude," Slocum said, watching the deputy go.

"He came with the job. He's the mayor's cousin," Bigelow said. "I wouldn't trust him to pour piss out of a boot."

He put his shotgun down, laying it on its side on the trestle table. He caught sight of the freshly opened bottle of tequila and licked his lips.

"Buy you a drink," Slocum said.

"Duty first," said Bigelow. He went to Sim Treece, who lay flat on his back with his eyes and mouth open. A long dark worm of blood clung to the side of his mouth.

Bigelow went to one knee, grunting. He searched the body, turning out Sim's pockets, fishing out a leather pouch with a drawstring mouth pulled closed. It was swollen with a nice hefty weight as he held it in the palm of one hand. It made clinking noises. He opened the top of the pouch, revealing a yellow gleam.

"Gold coins," Bigelow said husky-voiced, his narrow

eyes glittering. He glanced sideways at Slocum, appraising him.

"That's evidence," Slocum said. "You'd better take it into custody."

"Them's my thoughts," Bigelow said. He pulled the mouth of the pouch closed tight, then made the pouch disappear in an inside pocket.

He went through Brick's pockets, then Toby's, finding a couple of wads of greenbacks and a few coins and pocketing them. When there was nothing more to be found, he straightened up, rising heavily with a half groan, half sigh. He was sweating heavily, and his slitted eyes shone brighter than ever.

He lumbered out of the sun, into the shade of the patio. He took off his hat, wiped his sweaty forehead with the arm of his shirt, and put his hat back on.

Slocum poured tequila into both glasses and pushed one across the table to Bigelow. "Don't mind if I do," the sheriff said. They both drank and set down empty glasses.

"Ah," Bigelow said. "This is turning out to be a pretty good day after all."

"No kick about the Treece brothers?"

"The hell with 'em. They were troublemakers. Nobody'll miss 'em."

"Why do I have the feeling that you'd be saying the same thing about me if the situation was reversed and I was the one lying there shot dead?"

"Because you're smart," Bigelow said. "Like I told you before, I didn't take the job of being the law in this flyspeck county so's I could be a hero."

"Why did you take it, Dan?"

"Because I like eating regular. And because I wanted some peace and quiet."

"And then I showed up."

"That's right. What're you doing in Los Palos anyhow, Slocum?"

"Like I said, to meet a man."

"Who?"

"Fellow named Manfred."

"Manfred? Never heard of him. What's his game?"

"I don't rightly know, not yet. But I've got a feeling I'm going to find out soon," Slocum said. "Damned soon, unless I miss my guess."

As he spoke, Slocum was looking past Bigelow, toward the west side of the plaza, where a horse-drawn carriage flanked by a small band of riders came into view.

A six-horse team was yoked to the carriage, which was shiny black. It was the source of the second cloud of dust that had followed along the road in the wake of the Treece brothers.

Flanked by its handful of outriders, it rolled to a halt in front of the strip of hotels and saloons near the courthouse.

Bigelow said, "Who's that?"

"Manfred maybe," Slocum said.

"Don't you know?"

"Never met the man. A third party that I do know got word to me a while back that this Manfred was looking to maybe hire me on for a job, and that if I was interested, to meet him in Los Palos right around this time of the month."

"What kind of a job?"

Slocum gave him a bland look. "Maybe he wants me to lead a cattle drive or something," he said.

"That's a good one. There must be money in it, whatever it is, or you wouldn't be here. Nobody comes to a place like Los Palos without a damned good reason."

"Yeah? What's yours, Dan?"

"I wanted to loaf and get paid for it, and being sheriff

around here is the next best thing. Or at least it was,'' he said, glancing at the bodies.

"What do you care? You're making out all right,'' Slocum said.

"Yeah,'' Bigelow said, grinning. He patted the money pouch in his vest, and the coins made jolly little clinking sounds. "That's more than six months' wages.''

"You had a good day,'' Slocum said, "and it's early yet.''

"You figuring on more trouble?''

"Who knows? I wasn't even figuring on the Treece brothers.''

Bigelow parked his hip on the edge of table. The planks groaned under his weight. He pushed his empty glass forward. Slocum filled it.

"The brothers were killers for hire,'' Bigelow said. "Somebody paid 'em. Got any ideas who?''

Slocum shook his head. "There's plenty who'd like to see me dead, but none of them knew I was here in Los Palos.''

"Somebody did. Manfred maybe,'' Bigelow said, eyeing Slocum shrewdly.

"A man I don't know sends for me, then hires the Treeces to get rid of me? It don't figure,'' Slocum said.

Bigelow scratched his head, then his butt. "Well, it's all too deep for me. I'm just a simple country sheriff. As far as the law is concerned, the Treeces got what was coming. There'll be an inquest, just as soon as I can get enough citizens sobered up for a coroner's jury. But that's just a formality.

"By the way,'' he added too casually, "there won't be any need to go into the details of the case. That'd just confuse the simple souls we got around here. We'll just say the Treeces were gunning for you to make themselves a rep, only you got them. No need to testify about the money."

"What money?" Slocum said, blank-faced.

"Haw! I knew you and me were going to get along."

"Let's have a drink on it."

They did.

3

Now that the shooting was over and it was safe to come out, the folks of Los Palos came out. Even under that hot sun, they'd come out for a killing. For three killings, wild horses couldn't drag them away. They drifted to the scene, singly and in groups. The cantina owner was already there. He'd come back as soon as it was clear that the sheriff and the stranger weren't going to start blasting at each other. The owner disliked leaving his property unattended for too long. His wife and daughters were close behind him.

Bigelow sent a couple of flunkies to round up the dead men's horses. "They're mine now," he said, chuckling. He looked at Slocum for his reaction. Slocum's blank face remained unchanged. Bigelow chuckled some more.

People grouped around the bodies, forming a small crowd. There were store clerks and saloon girls, cowboys and kids. There was a kind of a festive mood in the air. Not much happened in Los Palos. This was a real break in the routine.

Somebody found a couple of old horse blankets, which were used to cover the bodies. They couldn't cover up the stink, though.

Slocum got tired of being gawked at, and started to move off. Bigelow said, "Where're you going?"

"Inside," Slocum said, indicating the cantina.

"Stay around. We'll have to hold an inquest, and this is as good a place as any. Better, because here you can get a drink. Hey, you forgot your bottle!"

The bottle was about a third full. "You keep it," Slocum said.

A big grin split Bigelow's whiskery moon face, a wolfish grin. "You're a pal. I wish more citizens cooperated with the law like you do."

"Law and order, that's me," Slocum said.

He went into the cantina. It took some seconds for his eyes to adjust to the dimness. The owner was bustling behind the bar. In the kitchen, the three females were whipping up a mess of victuals.

Slocum crossed to the bar. The coin that he'd left for the bottle was gone. He pointed to where it'd been, saying, "You found that *dinero*."

"Si, Señor, I found it. *Gracias*."

"De nada."

The owner set down a glass on the bar and poured a drink. "That one is on the house."

"Much obliged." Savory food smells tingled in his nose. "What's cooking?"

"Venison chili, Señor."

"Let me have a bowl of it."

The owner called for a bowl. It would be ready in a few minutes. Slocum took a bottle and a glass to a rear table in the corner. He sat with his back to the wall, facing the door.

People came in, going to the bar. Once they'd looked around and seen him, they generally made a point of looking elsewhere. They drank fast and hard, and that and the effects of the sun went to their heads. Soon there was plenty of loud talk and high spirits.

Slocum glanced at the kitchen, to see if his food was ready. He saw the owner's wife bending to get something out of a cabinet. Her back was to him, and when she leaned forward from the waist, her ass was outlined against her dark thin skirt, as big and round as a serving platter. She was middle-aged, with a figure like two sacks of potatoes, but he felt a stirring below the belt.

That always happened after a killing. He wanted, needed a woman. It was purely physical, a bodily craving. A hunger. Having cheated death, he wanted to grab hold of life with both hands, and there was nothing more lively than a naked woman between the sheets.

Then the woman stood up and turned around, showing a face like a shaved dish-faced bear, and Slocum's appetites shifted their focus above the waist, to his belly.

There were two daughters, both in their teens. The eldest was already hard-faced and thick-waisted, with two babies, but the younger was fresh, ripe. She brought out a plate with a bowl of chili and some squares of cornbread. There was high color in her face, and she didn't look directly at Slocum as she set down the plate and utensils. She was slim-hipped, with high, firm, pointed breasts that pressed against her thin white cotton blouse as she leaned forward over the table.

Slocum felt that tingling again. The girl set down the food and scurried away, padding gracefully on sandaled feet.

The chili made his mouth water. He grabbed a spoon and dug in.

He was just scraping the bowl clean and thinking of calling for a second helping when a figure loomed up in front of his table.

It was a man, tall, slender, thin-faced, with thick gray hair combed straight back from his forehead and covering his scalp like a leaden cap. He had a glossy silver eyebrow mustache. He dressed like a businessman, in a dark suit, white shirt, and dark tie. The tie had a fancy knot and a golden stickpin with a sunburst emblem that could have been a coat of arms. His pants were tucked into the tops of a pair of English-style riding boots. Something in his bearing suggested a military background, his posture, the way he held himself. He wore no side arms, but the bulge in his jacket in the right hand pocket was made by a pistol.

He said, "Mr. Slocum?"

"That's me."

The man nodded, dipping his head in a quick formal bow. "Allow me to introduce myself. I am Manfred."

"Then you're the fellow that sent for me," Slocum said, musing. "Sit down."

"Thank you." Manfred pulled out a chair and sat down across the table from Slocum. Slocum pushed the dirty dishes to the side, out of the way. The cantina was full now, with a couple dozen people. Slocum caught the server's eye and signaled her to come over.

He said, "What're you drinking?"

Manfred smiled thinly. "Thank you, no. It's a bit early in the day for me." He spoke correctly, but with a foreign accent, one which Slocum couldn't place.

The girl came over to the table and took away the dirty dishes. When she was gone, Manfred leaned forward, intent.

"It seems that you have just survived a most eventful encounter, Mr. Slocum. Three against one. I am glad to see that the reports of your prowess have not been exaggerated."

The smile widened, still with no warmth in it. "You have been well chosen for our enterprise. My principal will be pleased."

He pushed his head forward, raising an eyebrow, lowering his voice. "These men who tried to kill you—who were they?"

"The Treece brothers."

"Why did they try to kill you?"

"I was hoping you could tell me that."

Manfred shook his head, looking puzzled. "I know nothing of these men and their motives, and neither, I assure you, does my principal."

"They were killers for hire. They wouldn't have gone gunning for me if somebody hadn't paid them. Who? Not you, I figure."

"Certainly not!"

"They were in an all-fired hurry to kill me before you got here."

"I regret that I cannot be more candid with you until you've entered into a more formal arrangement with my principal, Mr. Slocum. Surely you can see the necessity of discretion. After all, confidentiality must be maintained in the event that you should decide not to enter into our forthcoming venture."

"When somebody tries to kill me, I want answers, friend."

Annoyance flickered over Manfred's face, but he stifled it, like a man holding back a sneeze. Clearly, he wasn't used to being addressed in so pointed a manner, and didn't like it.

"You have every right to feel the way you do, sir. I can tell you this. Our project is opposed by sinister forces who would kill to stop it."

"Thanks for telling me now. It's a little late, though."

"Your possible involvement in this business was closely held, Mr. Slocum, closely held." Now Manfred was frowning. "Its discovery is very worrisome. It could mean that we have a traitor in our camp, a spy. Unless, of course, you might perhaps have let slip an indiscreet word, some casual remark, strictly in passing?''

"I don't tell my business to strangers. Or friends either," Slocum said flatly.

"No, of course not. My apologies for even asking, but I must be thorough and investigate every possibility, no matter how remote. A traitor in our ranks—unthinkable! And yet, what else?

"I will find this Judas and kill him, I promise you that."

"Strong talk," Slocum said.

"Not talk, sir. A vow. I swear it."

"Well, you can't find him too soon, not as far as I'm concerned. I don't want anybody else coming after me. Not until after I've got a firm deal with you people."

Manfred's scowl relaxed into a faint sneering smile. "I was hoping you would not let all this dissuade you from joining us."

"That depends on the deal. When do we get down to brass tacks?"

Manfred stared, uncomprehending. "Talk business," Slocum said. "Getting down to brass tacks means to talk business."

"Ah, I see! One of your colorful Americanisms," Manfred said. "You must understand, I am only an agent, acting on behalf of my principal."

"Who's your principal, and when do I get to meet him?"

"Come to the Dorado Hotel tonight at eight. Your questions will be answered there."

"All right," Slocum said.

Manfred pushed back his chair and stood up. "A man who can kill three men and then sit down to a hearty lunch is a man who has my approval, sir. It shows that he doesn't have a weak stomach about killing, and that's the kind of man our enterprise needs.

"In any case, you'll be expected at eight. Good day."

His head bobbed in a whippy little bow. Then Manfred turned on his heel and started off, just as Bigelow was starting toward the table. Manfred brushed past the sheriff and wove through the crowd, exiting out the door.

"Who's that?" Bigelow said, nodding toward the door.

"I don't know. Some foreigner," Slocum said.

4

Bigelow called the inquest to order, pounding on the table. He didn't have a gavel, so he used his fist. It was a big fist, the tabletop groaning under the blows.

"All right, *shaddup*! That's better. And no more drinking till the inquest is over," Bigelow said.

"That'll get it over in a hurry," he added.

He sat at the middle of a long table set lengthwise along the cantina's south wall. To his left sat the twelve men of the coroner's jury, twelve adult male citizens of Los Palos that Bigelow had corralled at random. They were grouped in two rows of six chairs each, set apart from the rest of the onlookers, who crowded the tables and chairs and the space around them. Slocum sat in front of the long table, a few paces away, facing Bigelow at an angle. Virgil, the deputy, stood crouching at one end of the long table.

The noisy chattering of the spectators faded to a murmur, then fell silent as Bigelow looked around, trying to see who was talking.

"This court is now in session," Bigelow said.

The undertaker doubled as the town coroner. He testified first, stating that the decedents were indeed dead, that they had guns in their hands, and that they had all been shot in front.

"And derned good shooting too," he added.

That took about two minutes. Then Slocum was sworn, with his hand on a bible. Bigelow ran the proceedings, and asked what few questions there were.

"What happened, Slocum?"

"The Treece brothers tried to get me, but I got them first."

Bigelow nodded. "No more questions." He turned to the jury, saying, "It's a hot day and there's no sense in anybody doing a lot of moving around that you don't have to do, so there's no need for the jury to retire. You can just give me your verdict of self-defense right here."

The jury members glanced at each other. "And don't take all day about it," Bigelow said. "We got a lot of thirsty folks waiting here, me included."

The jury foreman began, "We find a verdict of—"

"Stand up," Bigelow said. "Show some respect for the court."

"Sorry," the foreman said, rising. "We find a verdict of self-defense, and good riddance to the Treeces!"

"So found," Bigelow said, hammering the table with his fist. "Name your poison, boys and girls, because the court is buying one on the house!"

A cheer went up, followed by a rush to the bar. The undertaker lingered, saying, "What about the bodies, Dan?"

"Bury them, what else?"

"Maybe I should wire their hometown, see if anybody wants to finance a funeral."

"Don't bother. Dead killers have no friends. Plant 'em on Boot Hill and to hell with 'em."

Seeing the other's hesitation, Bigelow said, "The town's paying for it."

"Right," the undertaker said, now smiling.

"Nothing fancy," Bigelow cautioned. "Just plain pine boxes, the cheapest you got."

The undertaker stopped smiling. "What the hell, Dan? What do you care? It's not like the money's coming out of your pocket."

"You're damned right it's not. But I'm the one who's got to listen to the mayor and town council bitching about the price."

The undertaker leaned in, lowering his voice. "Maybe we could arrange a little fee-splitting on this job, eh, Dan? I scratch your back, you scratch my back?"

"Okay," Bigelow said, nodding vigorously. "But keep the price reasonable so there won't be too much squawking." He glanced at Slocum, who stood waiting nearby.

"Who knows, maybe there'll be a few more," he said.

"I sure hope so," the undertaker said. "That way we can both make a little money. Well, I'd better get to work. Those boys won't last, not in this hot weather."

He crossed to the door, exiting. Bigelow beckoned Slocum, signaling him to come over.

"Hear that, Slocum? There goes one citizen who thinks you're good for business."

"I'm always a big favorite with the undertakers."

"I'll bet," Bigelow said. He saw the deputy lurking around at the sidelines. "What're you doing sucking around, Virgil?"

"N-nothing, Sheriff."

"Go do it somewhere else. Scram—or do you need a boot in the tail to send you on your way?"

"No, sir! I'm going!"

He went—to the bar. "Sneaky little bastard," Bigelow said. "I'm afraid Virgil's starting to get big ideas."

"Maybe he smells money," Slocum said.

"Maybe."

"Too bad for him."

"A dirty shame," Bigelow agreed. "I guess I can stand it, though."

"Generous of you to buy everyone a drink."

"Just showing my appreciation to our public-spirited citizens. Besides, I can afford it," Bigelow said, tapping his shirt pocket where it held the gold coins.

He winked, leering. "Maybe there's more where that came from, huh? Maybe even from that fancy furriner you were talking to."

"Now who's getting big ideas?" Slocum said.

If the jab stung Bigelow, he didn't show it, the laugh lines remaining undiminished around his eyes.

"Big ideas? Not me, I'm just a simple country sheriff."

Slocum laughed.

5

Slocum was staying at the Dorado Hotel, the best lodgings in town. That wasn't saying much. It wasn't much of a town. After lunch, he went to the hotel. It was located a block or two west of the courthouse.

In front of the building was a veranda, about three feet off the ground. It was roofed over by the second-floor balcony. A couple of chairs for the use of the hotel guests stood on the shady front porch.

At the right corner of the porch stood two men, attired just like Manfred. They were young, fit, alert. One wore a brown suit, and the other a gray suit. Their pants were worn outside their boots. They both wore bowler hats. No guns were showing.

At the left corner stood a third man, dressed like the others, except his suit was dark brown. He had curly black hair and a set of tricky side-whiskers. He was rolling a long thin cigar in his fingers, not smoking it, just meditatively rolling it. It looked like a black pencil.

All three sets of eyes focused on Slocum as he approached the front of the hotel. The two men on the right put their heads together, talking in low tones, glancing at him.

Slocum climbed three wooden steps to the porch, then crossed to the front entrance. The trio made no move to interfere with him or do anything else but take note of his presence. They were just watching.

The watching wasn't all one-sided. Slocum did a little of his own. He noticed that the man with the side-whiskers wore a holstered gun under his coat, high up on his right waist. The rig was made of shiny black leather with a button-down flap. It looked military, like cavalry-issue. Not U.S. cavalry, though.

Slocum went into the hotel lobby. The carpets were frayed, the wooden floor was unpolished, and the furniture had seen better days. Off to one side, a man sat in an armchair facing the door, reading a newspaper. He held it in front of him with both hands, so it covered his face. On the drum table beside him was a bowler hat.

The desk clerk had seen better days too. He was as worn and frayed at the edges as the hotel furniture. He was balding, with baggy watery blue eyes.

"I'm gonna get some sleep," Slocum said. "Send somebody up to knock on my door at six o'clock."

"Yes, sir," the clerk said dully. Slocum slid a coin across the counter to him. "Thank you, sir!" said the clerk a little more brightly.

At the far end of the hotel, on the second-floor landing, a projecting balcony or gallery overlooked the lobby. Now, as Slocum stood leaning across the front desk, a woman came into view on the gallery. She stood at the balustrade, hands resting on the rail, coolly surveying the scene below.

She was in her early twenties, about five and a half feet tall, and well built, with an hourglass figure. A mass of brick-red hair was casually piled at the top of her head. She had a wide heart-shaped face with bold features and full lips. She wore a blue satin dress, unbuttoned at the collar to bare her neck and throat. Her skin was a tawny golden color.

Slocum eyed her, trying not to stare. "Looks like you've got some new guests at the hotel."

"Um," the clerk said, barely glancing up from his work to see whom Slocum meant.

"Who is she?"

"She's with the Valerian party. They've taken a number of rooms in the hotel."

"She's a good-looking woman."

"If you say so, sir. I hadn't noticed."

"You've been behind that desk too long," Slocum said.

The woman glanced in his direction. He touched the tip of his hat, but her only acknowledgment was to look away.

A man came out and stood beside her, a big six-footer with blond hair and a clean-shaven chiseled face. He was broad-shouldered and lean-hipped, in expensive clothes that were tailored to show off his physique. He wore a gun low on his hip, Western-style.

The redhead greeted his arrival with no more reaction than she had displayed to Slocum. The newcomer looked down into the lobby, scowling when he saw Slocum. He spoke to the redhead, taking her by the arm and drawing her away. She shrugged, turning, and allowed him to lead her off the balcony. She walked away, hips swaying, wiggling a ripe heart-shaped ass that was outlined under the blue dress.

"Whew," Slocum said. "Is she married?"

"I'm quite sure I don't know, sir."

"She sure doesn't walk like she's married."

"It's not my place to speculate about our guests, sir."

"Why not? I gave you a coin, didn't I? What do you want, another one? Okay, here it is."

"Really, sir, I couldn't—"

The flat ring of a coin being slapped down on the counter silenced the clerk's objections. He made the coin disappear.

"Er, I believe that the lady in question is the personal maid of Mrs. Valerian. Her room adjoins Mrs. Valerian's suite. Sorry, but I don't know her name."

"And this Mrs. Valerian, who's she?"

"Apparently she's the widow of a financier from back East. Her references are impeccable. They'd have to be, to satisfy our manager."

"A rich widow, eh? Is she good-looking?"

"Extremely attractive, if I may say so, sir."

"You may. That smooth-faced blond dude, who's he?"

"I believe that's a Mr. Wardell, a business associate of Mrs. Valerian."

"They sharing a room together?"

"Please, sir! This is a respectable hotel."

"I'll see what I can do to fix that," Slocum said. "That's a joke, so you can stop standing there looking like I spiked the punch at the church social.

"Is a fella named Manfred part of the bunch?"

The clerk relaxed, now on safer ground. "Indeed he is. A very fine gentleman, Mr. Manfred."

"And these other dudes hanging around the hotel, the ones with the bowler hats?"

"Yes, they're part of the Valerian group."

"Quite a party," Slocum said. "Don't forget about sending somebody to wake me at six o'clock."

"I won't, sir."

Slocum started toward the stairs, his path taking him past the man with the newspaper. The top of the paper was held below the man's eyes, so he could watch Slocum talking with the clerk. Now that Slocum was on the move, the man raised the paper to once more hide his face.

"It's okay, Manfred knows me," Slocum said to him in an aside. The man made no response.

The staircase was broken by a couple of landings. Slocum climbed it. At the top, a faint sweet, musky scent hung in the air, a trace of the redhead's perfume. Slocum took a couple of deep breaths, filling his lungs with it.

The woman was gone, and so was the hard-faced Wardell. Beyond the gallery, at the far end of a central corridor running the length of the second floor, a man sat in a straight-backed wooden chair that stood against the wall.

This was no bowler-hatted dude. This was an oversized bruiser with a hairless scalp and a thick, fierce black mustache. Massive shoulders started below his ears, swelling to the breadth of an ax handle. He was about 250 pounds of bulging muscle, dwarfing the chair he sat on so it looked like a piano stool. His big arms were folded across his chest. His dark eyes were like black buttons of coal as he stared straight ahead.

Slocum's room was on the left side of the hall, near the landing. He liked to stay close to the front, where he could keep tabs on what was happening in the lobby below. He took out his key and unlocked the door.

At the other end of the corridor, a door on the left opened, and out stepped Wardell, crossing to a door on the right. He took no notice of the big bald man, and the other took no notice of him, but kept solidly staring straight ahead.

Wardell rapped on the door, giving it a couple of sharp knocks. He saw Slocum and scowled. Slocum's door was unlocked and partly open, but he didn't enter, just stood there with a hand on the knob, eyeing Wardell.

Wardell gave him one of those what-the-hell-are-you-looking-at looks. Then the door on which he'd knocked was opened. From inside the room came the sound of female voices. Wardell entered, giving Slocum a dirty look before closing the door.

The bald mustached strongman kept staring straight ahead.

Slocum went into his room, locking the door. The window was open, but the air was close. The chambermaid had cleaned the room and made the bed. On a cabinet there was a pitcher of water and two glasses. Slocum drank from the pitcher, his throat working. When he set it down, the water was mostly gone.

He took off his shirt and his boots and socks. His torso was lean and hard, bronzed except for the ghostly white marks of old scars and bullet holes. He moved the bed aside, so it was outside the line of fire of the door.

He lay down on his back on the bed, on top of the covers, facing the door. His arms were at his sides, a gun in one hand. He dropped off into a restless, sweaty sleep, swarming with scraps of dreams of gold, guns, and women.

6

Slocum ate dinner in a small cafe two blocks south of the hotel. There were some tables and chairs and a short bar. There were only a few people at the bar, but all the tables were full. Slocum sat by himself at a round table that wasn't much bigger than his place setting. He had a steak, baked potato, salad, and hot biscuits. The food was decent. There was a restaurant in the hotel, but the food was lousy. And overpriced.

Earlier, when he'd woken from his nap, he'd wanted to take a bath, but the desk clerk had told him that all the hot water was being used by the Valerian crowd. So he'd gone to a public bathhouse and scrubbed himself clean in a hot steaming tub. He'd kept a gun at hand, but there hadn't been any trouble. A soaking had helped him sweat away his hangover, and after that and a shave, he felt pretty good. Then he'd gone to get something to eat.

Now, his belly was nicely full, but not so much so that he didn't have room for apple pie and coffee. While he was waiting for the waitress to return, he stared out the window, watching long shadows slant and slide across the street. The sky was still light, and it was still hot, but nowhere near as brutal as it had been at midday.

At the bar were three young toughs, locals, from the looks of them. They all wore guns. They drank fast and often, and talked loud and laughed louder. The few others who'd been at the bar when they had arrived had soon drifted off elsewhere.

Slocum drew his knife from its boot sheath and laid it flat on the table, near his right hand. He didn't fuss. He just took it out, laid it on the table, and went back to looking out the window.

The troublemakers got louder, more rowdy. It wasn't a saloon, it was a cafe, and the patrons didn't care for this kind of horseplay. The barkeep had a worried look. He had an egg-shaped head, with inky-black thinning hair plastered straight down, and a pair of curled mustachios looking like two commas lying on their sides.

The youngsters' language got rougher. An older couple stiffened, abruptly standing up, leaving their meals half finished. The man threw some coins on the table and he and the woman stalked out, stiff-necked. The rowdies gave them a big horselaugh. The other patrons ignored what was going on and ate faster, heads down, shoveling food into their mouths.

Slocum glanced back toward the kitchen, where the waitress was taking a long time bringing the rest of his order. Come to think of it, she hadn't come out of the kitchen since the three loudmouths had started making noise. Not that he blamed her for not wanting to run the gauntlet past the troublemakers. But he sure had a hankering for that pie, and he could smell the coffee.

Then, as he'd expected, the loudest of the three toughs started swaggering his way. He was skinny, with a mean pimply face. He wore a black hat and a fancy black holster with silver studs and a big fancy gun.

His followers hung a pace behind him. The fancy-gunned punk hooked his thumbs in the top of his gun belt and stood sneering down at Slocum.

"So you're the red-hot who gunned down the Treece brothers," he said. "You must be pretty fast."

"Ask them," Slocum said.

"Think you're faster'n me, mister?"

The people at the nearby tables got up and hurried out the front door. The punk's sneer widened as he saw the foot-long knife on the table.

"What the hell's that for?"

"I'm gonna use it to split your gizzard," Slocum said.

The pair on the sidelines suddenly stopped smirking and tried to make themselves look small, but their pal didn't see that. He was too busy trying to stare down Slocum. It wasn't Slocum who'd put the fear into the others; it was what they saw looming up on the pimple-faced kid, what he couldn't see because his back was to the front door.

Sheriff Bigelow had just marched through the swinging double doors, and was bearing down fast on light noiseless feet.

He clapped a hand on the kid's shoulder and spun him around, growling, "Dammit, Dennis, I told you what would happen the next time you made trouble."

Before Dennis could reply, Bigelow kneed him between the legs. Dennis's eyes widened as if they were going to pop out of his head. Bigelow backhanded him across the mouth, then smacked him coming the other way around, big meaty chops that sent the kid's head twisting around as if his neck was made of rags.

Bigelow pulled Dennis's gun from the holster and tossed it aside. He collared him at the back of the neck. If he hadn't been holding him up, Dennis would have collapsed.

Bigelow looked around, his gaze sweeping across Dennis's pals. Their eyes widened and their hands shot up palms out, to show they were harmless. Bigelow caught sight of a nearby window, and he started waltzing Dennis toward it, sweeping him across the floor so the youth's boot toes were the only part of him touching boards.

The barkeep cried, "Sheriff, please, not the window!"

Bigelow was about to stuff Dennis headfirst through the window, but stopped abruptly, changing course toward the entrance. At the threshold, he applied his own boot toe to Dennis's butt, in a kick that sent Dennis flying out the double doors.

Slocum heard the thump as Dennis flopped into the dirt street.

It had all taken a handful of seconds. Bigelow glanced at Dennis's pals, who stood cowering. "You're still here?" he said.

They ran out the door and away, ignoring their fallen comrade. Dennis lay curled on his side in the street, holding himself between the legs, his purple fish face gasping for air.

Bigelow brushed off his palms, not even having broken a sweat. He went outside, into the street. When Dennis saw him coming he tried to wriggle away, squirming like an earthworm.

Bigelow raised a foot to stomp him, then saw Virgil standing on the other side of the street. He put the foot down and said, "C'mere, you."

Virgil slunk over, cowering. Bigelow put his fists on his meaty hips.

"What're you doing, Virgil, following me?"

"Hell, no, Sheriff! I heard there was trouble at the cafe, so I came to see what I could do."

Bigelow nudged Dennis with his boot toe. "You can take this piece of trash over to the jail and throw his ass in a cell, that's what you can do."

Virgil leaned forward, trying to see the face of the beaten

punkeen. "Why, that's Dennis Rance—Jardeen's nephew!"

"So what?"

"Jardeen won't like this!"

"Well, ain't that just too bad," Bigelow said, his voice thick with sarcasm. "If he wants to kick about it, he knows where to find me. Okay, Deputy, move that prisoner out.

"And he'd better be in the lockup when I get there, unless you want some of what he got."

Bigelow turned and went into the cafe, crossing to Slocum's table. "Pull up a chair and sit down," Slocum said.

"Don't mind if I do." He did.

"Buy you a drink."

"Make it a bottle."

"All right," Slocum said. He raised his hand to signal the barkeep, but that worthy was already coming out from behind the bar with a bottle of whiskey.

"No charge, Sheriff," he said, after setting the bottle down on the table.

"Thanks," Bigelow said gruffly.

"Thank *you*," the barkeep said, turning to go.

Slocum said, "Hey, where's my apple pie and coffee?"

"I'll see about it myself. Any friend of Sheriff Dan's . . ." The barkeep hurried off into the kitchen.

"Who was that?" Slocum said.

"Who, Ollie? He runs the cafe."

"Not him, the kid."

"Who, the punk? That's Dennis Rance. His uncle's Jardeen, so he thinks he's fast."

"Jerry Jardeen? He is fast."

"You know him?"

"We've met."

Bigelow eyed him shrewdly. "That have anything to do with why you're in Los Palos?"

"No. I didn't even know he was in these parts."

"He comes and goes. One of these days he's gonna come around here once too often. He's another troublemaker I don't need.

"As for his nephew, he's a snot-nosed kid who's too big for his britches. I told him that the next time I had a run-in with him, I'd stomp him flat. Thirty days of breaking hard rocks in the hot sun for the county should take some of the starch out of him."

The barkeep returned with a quart pot of coffee and a big slice of pie. Bigelow called for another mug. He cracked the seal on the fresh bottle of liquor, held it under his nose, and inhaled, as if he was smelling the perfume of a flower.

"Ahh, bottled in bond. Ollie knows how to treat me right," he said, smacking his lips. He splashed a fat slug of whiskey in the bottom of the mug, and filled the rest with hot black coffee.

"Have a taste."

"Sure," Slocum said. "But make it a light one. I'm still shaking off my last hangover."

"Hair of the dog," Bigelow said, pouring. "Say, that pie looks pretty good."

"It is good," Slocum said between mouthfuls.

"Hey, Ollie, bring us a couple more pieces of pie," Bigelow called. Ollie brought most of what was left of a whole pie, plus a fork and plate. Bigelow dug in, and for a few moments talk ceased while he and Slocum wielded their forks.

Finally coming up for air, Bigelow said, "As a matter of fact, Slocum, I been looking for you."

"Oh?"

Bigelow pulled out a money pouch and set it down on the table, pushing it toward Slocum. "Here."

"What's that?"

"Your share of the money from the Treece boys. Go on, take it."

Slocum raised an eyebrow. "Not that I don't like money, but why so generous?"

Bigelow shrugged. "Why be greedy? I mean, what the hell, you killed 'em. I figure you're entitled to make something on the deal. That way there's no hard feelings."

Slocum made no move toward the pouch. Bigelow pushed it closer to him, saying, "G'wan, take it, don't make me out to be a piker."

"What's in it for you?"

"Funny you should ask," Bigelow said, beaming with genial corruption. "I ain't blind. I can see that something's going on. First you blow in out of nowhere, a top gun wasting time in this one-horse town. Then the Treece brothers come gunning for you, with real gold in their pockets. Their bodies have barely hit the ground when this bunch of fancy foreigners rides in and takes over the top floor of the Dorado Hotel. You're staying at the Dorado, ain't 'cha?"

"Yeah."

"How about that?" Bigelow leaned forward, his voice lower. "I know the signs. Something's cooking. The only thing I can't figure out is what. There's nothing in Los Palos worth stealing. I know. The pickings in these parts are so slim that it almost pays better to be honest."

"Don't get carried away now," Slocum said.

"All right, I'm exaggerating, but not much. The money in the bank's not worth the powder to blow it up. So what is it? A lost gold mine? Gunrunning across the border? A little revolution planned down Mexico way? What?"

"I don't know."

Bigelow sank back in his seat, smiling sourly. "Aw, now, here we got a problem. I'm leveling with you and you're holding out. Is that nice?"

"I'm not holding out. I don't know myself."

"Tell me another."

"All I know is that a certain party wants to hire me for a job. You know me, so you know it's not a job digging fence posts or herding cattle. I got a little money in advance, enough to pay for my time and trouble to come down to Los Palos for a meeting. The meeting's tonight, in less than an hour.

"Now you know what I know. Why? You want in?"

"We'd make a good team, you and me, Slocum."

"I thought you liked sitting on the right side of the law."

"I thought so too, till today. Man, there's been more action here in one day than in the last six months. It put the taste for it in my mouth. I'm getting stale here, rousting drunks and slapping around wet-behind-the-ears punks. I'd like to make some real money."

Slocum flicked the pouch with a fingertip, making the coins jingle. "And yet you're giving it away."

"I told you I ain't blind. I ain't dumb either. If the Treeces are being paid in gold to get you, then the big prize, the one that's worth killing for, must be really big," said Bigelow, grinning.

"Okay," Slocum said, reaching for the pouch and dropping it into an inside vest pocket.

"Partners?" Bigelow said.

"Let's see what the deal is. If it looks good, we're partners. If not, I'll give you the money back."

"You're damned right you will," Bigelow said. "Think I'll have me another piece of pie."

7

At eight o'clock Slocum started down the long hall on the second floor of the Dorado Hotel. The bald brute with the fierce mustache was still sitting at his post at the opposite end of the hall. He stood up when Slocum had passed the halfway mark along the corridor. He took up a lot of space. He took a few paces forward and halted, standing with hands on hips and legs spread, in a posture that said that nobody was getting by him.

"Ah! There you are, Mr. Slocum," said Manfred, who was coming up behind him at a brisk pace. "I was waiting for you in the lobby, but you must have come in when I stepped away for a moment."

He fell into step beside Slocum, speaking a few words to the sentry in a language unknown to Slocum.

The sentry nodded, his glowering undiminished as he stepped back, out of the way.

"He's a big one," Slocum said. "He doesn't say much, does he?"

"The Turk is a man of few words," said Manfred. He paused in front of a door on the right, the one which Slocum had seen Wardell enter earlier. He opened the door, Slocum following him inside.

The room was actually a suite, a series of rooms. The front room was a kind of drawing room. At the center was a dark wooden octagonal table with some straight-backed chairs grouped around it. Along the walls were other pieces of overstuffed furniture, some seedy armchairs, and a divan. The room was lit with globe oil lamps, which gave a yellow tint to the peeling cream-colored walls and ceiling. The shoulder-high wooden wainscoting and moldings were dark brown; the carpeting was a muddy wine color. Opposite the door to the hall, at the other end of the room, a closed door was set in the wall. It was flanked by a pair of doors in the sidewalls that met it at tilted angles. They were closed too.

Apart from Slocum and Manfred, the only other occupant of the drawing room was the man whom Slocum had seen earlier reading a newspaper in the hotel lobby. Now, he was reading a *Police Gazette*. He put it down and rose when he saw Manfred. He wasn't exactly standing at attention, but it was something like it. Manfred said, "That will be all, Kurt."

"I will be downstairs in the room with the others, Captain," said Kurt. He picked up his magazine and went out the hall door.

"Captain?" Slocum said.

Manfred showed his teeth in a thin smile. He had good teeth. "At one time I was an officer, but I have since resigned my commission. My men continue to use the title, however, through force of habit."

"Officer in what army? If you don't mind my asking."

"Not at all, though I feel the answer will mean little to you. I once had the honor of serving with the Imperial Palace Guards of the principality of Hyundagar."

"Never heard of it."

"I would be surprised if you had. It is a tiny but proud

principality which lies between the land of the Bulgars and Hungary.''

"That's in Europe, right?''

"Quite so.''

"You're a long way from home.''

"Quite so,'' Manfred repeated, this time with a trace of melancholy. With a physical effort he shook away the mood, bustling around to a sideboard on which stood a cut-crystal decanter and some goblets. "May I offer you something to drink, Mr. Slocum?''

"Sure, as long as it's not water.''

"The manager of the hotel assures me that this is the finest brandy of the house's stock. At that, it's not too bad. Amazing to find a decent brandy at all in this benighted land!

"But I beg pardon if I have given offense. It is not seemly for an outlander to criticize when he is a guest in your country.''

"It doesn't bother me. I'm from Georgia myself.''

"Ah, yes, that is in your American Southland, is it not? Then you too are a long way from home.''

Manfred uncapped the decanter and poured some of the reddish-amber liquid in two goblets. He and Slocum raised their glasses.

"To absent homelands,'' Manfred said.

"Home is where I hang my hat.''

"An admirable sentiment, sir. A soldierly sentiment. Your health, sir, and the success of our enterprise.''

"I'll drink to that.''

Manfred took a mouthful of brandy. Slocum tossed his back in a gulp, drawing a line of liquid heat down his throat that exploded in a bonfire in the pit of his belly.

He set down the empty glass, saying, "And now, what's the game? And who's paying for it?''

"I am,'' said a voice. A woman's voice. Its owner stood

in the now-open doorway of the middle of the three doors. She was tall, slim, straight, high-breasted, and long-legged. Her hair was bronze-colored, thick, and straight, hanging to her shoulders like a helmet. Her eyes were a hazel color so light that they seemed brownish-gold. Her skin was ivory. She had high cheekbones, a sharp narrow nose, and full lips. Her gaze was cool, level.

She wore a brown jacket with black velvet collar and cuffs, a matching brown ankle-length skirt, and small elegant boots with pointed toes and high heels. At her throat was a spray of lace and an oval cameo in a heavy gold setting. Pinned over her left breast was a massy gold starburst medallion, a larger version of the device that Manfred wore as a stickpin.

The tunic-style jacket fit tightly, outlining a full rounded bosom and lean torso. Her hips were nicely rounded too, atop long legs. Her face was beautiful but cold, lips compressed in a tight line that could indicate strong emotions strongly controlled.

Slocum was glad that he'd taken a bath and put on clean clothes. He was less glad when he saw Wardell emerge from the room she had just left. Wardell didn't seem too happy to see him either.

Manfred drew himself up, subtly clicking his heels. "I have the honor to present the Baroness Mala Valerian, of the House of Rao in Hyundagar." He said it as if it meant something important.

"Baroness, allow me to introduce Mr. Slocum," Manfred said.

"Ah, yes, the celebrated gunfighter," she said, skirts rustling softly as she came deeper into the room, extending her hand as Slocum crossed to her.

He took her hand, dipping his head in a courtly bow and lightly, very lightly, kissing her hand. "Charmed, Baroness."

"You are gallant, sir," she said, seeming a bit surprised.

"If there's one thing we Georgia boys learn at our mothers' knees, it's manners," Slocum said.

"You can let go of her hand now," Wardell said.

Slocum released his grip, turning toward Wardell with a blandly pleasant expression on his face. The corners of Manfred's mouth quirked upward, amused by the air of instant hostility that had sprung up between the two men.

"Mr. Slocum, Mr. Wardell," he said. From his tone, he wasn't overly enamored of Wardell either.

Wardell went to the sideboard and poured himself a drink, avoiding having to shake hands. His back was to Slocum as he tossed back a shot, shuddering.

Slocum said, "Glad to know you, Wardell."

"Yeah?"

"Not really. I was just being polite."

Wardell turned slowly, facing him. He was a handsome man with a mean face. His eyes were the color of blueberries, his chiseled face ruddy.

"I don't think I'm going to like you, Slocum."

Slocum smiled with his lips, seemingly undisturbed. "I don't have to like a man to work with him, as long as the price is right. But who's paying the freight, you or the baroness?"

Wardell opened his mouth to say something, and from the look on his face it would've been something nasty, but before he could speak, the baroness said, "You will be working for me, Mr. Slocum."

"I haven't said I will work for you, but at least that's one point in your favor."

Wardell's face reddened, and he took a step forward, saying, "Listen, you—"

The baroness silenced him with an upraised hand. "Please, Arlen, don't be tiresome. Mr. Slocum is my guest, and I won't tolerate rudeness to those who enjoy my hospitality.''

Wardell swallowed his irritation and backed off. ''I'm just trying to keep you from wasting your money, Mala.''

''And I appreciate it, dear. But you must allow me to handle my business arrangements as I see fit,'' the baroness said. Her English was precise and accentless, but that very precision and careful enunciation made it sound foreign.

Wardell shrugged and with dark-faced ill grace, went to the sideboard and built himself another drink.

The baroness said, ''Please join me at table.'' She went to sit down. Wardell started toward her chair, but Slocum was there first, pulling the chair away from the octagonal table, then easing it forward after she had seated herself. Wardell quickly occupied the chair on her right. Slocum took the chair on the left. Manfred sat opposite the baroness, his back to the hall door.

''I understand you have already experienced some unpleasantness this day, Mr. Slocum.''

''It was the other fellows who got the worst of it, Baroness.''

''There were three of them, Manfred tells me. Killers.''

''They *were*.''

She nodded, eyes half-closed, a half-smile on her lips. ''That is good. Now more than ever, I am convinced that you are the man for the job.''

''What job is that, Baroness?''

Her eyes opened, then narrowed. They were long eyes, slightly upturned at the corners, giving them a catlike appearance. Her gaze turned inward, while she chewed the edges of her mouth. Slocum guessed that she was thinking over how much to tell him.

''I must speak of secret matters, but before I do so, I must have your pledge that these matters will remain secret.''

"If you know who I am, then you know that I know how to keep my mouth shut, Baroness."

"Yes . . . Shackleton and Newcolm both swore that you could be trusted implicitly."

Slocum nodded. Shackleton was a wealthy mining magnate in Arizona, and Newcolm was a major shareholder in the Denver and Rio Grande Railroad. Both had had problems, Shackleton with a gang of gold thieves, Newcolm with wreckers in the pay of a competing rail line. After they had hired Slocum, their problems had gone away— and six feet under.

"Strictly speaking, this may involve a question of, er, legality," she said.

"I'm not overly concerned with legal niceties. Shackleton and Newcolm must've told you that."

"There was some discussion in that vein, all in the most discreet and circumspect manner, of course."

"Of course," echoed Slocum, smiling sardonically. Both jobs had involved killing. Justified killing, but killing all the same. Neither businessman was liable to shout his connections to Slocum from the rooftops.

"Let's put our cards on the table, Baroness," Slocum said. "I'm already involved in your business up to my neck, whatever it is. The Treece Brothers, the three I killed, didn't come after me because of *my* business. They came after me because of *your* business. We're already yoked together in somebody's eyes."

Wardell shot Slocum a nasty glance. "I'm not sure I care for your turn of phrase, mister."

The baroness said, "What troubles me is how they could have known of it."

"I'm afraid our security has been compromised, Your Ladyship," Manfred said.

"But how can that be?"

Manfred shrugged. "A chance remark passed in the wrong ears . . . who knows?"

One of Wardell's hands was wrapped around his drink, the other resting on the table. That latter hand now became a fist.

"I've said all along that it was foolish to bring any outsiders into this," he said.

"Not being of the house of Rao, you too might be considered an outsider," said Manfred with some tartness.

"I'll let Mala be the judge of that," Wardell said.

The baroness covered Wardell's fist with one of her own slim hands and squeezed it fondly, draining some of the tension from him.

"You know my feelings for you, Arlen," she said warmly.

Some lingering doubt in his eyes betrayed that his suspicions might not be entirely quieted, but the rest of his face was loose, relaxed, smiling.

Slocum pushed back his chair and rose, the other three at the table staring up at him. Wardell smiled nastily, saying, "Going somewhere?"

"Just to get a drink. This fencing around is thirsty work."

"Pray, sit down and do not trouble yourself, Mr. Slocum. My servant will fetch us some refreshments."

"I don't mind getting it myself, Baroness—"

"Please, sit. You are my guest, and besides, that is what servants are for," she said. *"Lorelei."*

"Coming, milady," Lorelei said, entering the room by the door through which the baroness had come.

Lorelei was the redhead whom Slocum had seen earlier talking on the gallery with Wardell. She still wore the blue dress, with its low-cut neckline showing a lot of skin. It was skin worth showing, the rounded tops of her breasts and a deep cleavage.

"This is Lorelei, my personal maid and confidante since childhood. I have no secrets from her," the baroness said. "Not the way she listens at the keyhole."

"I was not listening at the door. I was watching. To see the handsome stranger," Lorelei said. Her English was more strongly accented than her mistress's. It had a husky, singsong quality.

"This is Mr. Slocum, Lorelei. He's deciding whether to come in with us on a business venture. If he does, you'll get to know him much better, I'm sure."

"I'm sure, Baroness."

"Intimately, one might say."

"One might."

"Bah!" Wardell said, with a face of disgust.

"Mr. Wardell is out of temper tonight," Lorelei said.

"Mr. Wardell would never do, or say, anything not befitting a gentleman," the baroness said, speaking not to the maid but to Wardell.

Lorelei went to the sideboard and picked up the decanter. The baroness said, "None for me, thanks. You may serve our other guests."

Lorelei went to Slocum, standing beside him as she leaned over with the decanter to pour him a refill. Her chest was inches from his face. He eyed her breasts with a long sidelong glance, staring so hard his eyes crossed. The next thing he knew, she was moving away from him and his glass was full.

He noticed that a fine sheen of sweat had broken out on his forehead.

Lorelei moved around the table. Manfred declined a drink. Wardell took the decanter from Lorelei's hands, saying, "I've already seen the peep show. I'll pour it myself."

She shrugged. He refilled his glass, setting the decanter down on the table in front of him.

"You can leave the bottle," he said.

The baroness nodded. "You've already served as enough distraction for one night, Lorelei. Go about your duties in the other room."

"Yes, milady."

"With the door closed. And no peeking!"

"Yes, milady." Lorelei crossed behind the baroness to the open doorway, moving with an easy, loose-limbed grace, like a big cat. Her hips swayed and her blue satin dress rustled. She went into the room, closing the door behind her, the latch clicking.

Wardell took a big gulp of brandy. His face got redder, but that was the only visible change. Slocum sipped his drink, slowing down. Best not to get too much of a skinful, not with these cagey characters.

The baroness put both her hands palms-flat down on the table. "So, now to business."

"It's your play," Slocum said.

"This is a delicate matter to broach. I have your word that what we speak of will go no farther than this room?"

"No."

The others hadn't been expecting that answer, and it gave them something of a turn. They weren't sure how to react. Now that Slocum had broken up their timing, he bored in.

"I can't give you my word on something I can't control. I can give you my word that I won't talk about it, and that's all," he said.

Manfred stiffened. Wardell looked down in his glass, swirling around the spoonful of brandy left in the bottom. Not looking up, he said mildly, "You saying one of us can't be trusted?"

"I'm saying that your secret's already out," Slocum said, speaking to the baroness. "You people are trying to lock up the barn door after the horse's been stolen. Whoever hired the Treece brothers to kill me did so to wreck your plans. You'd know who that might be better than I would.''

A quick glance was exchanged between the others, prompting Slocum to believe that they did have some common antagonist in mind.

He said, ''Like it or not, I'm already in. I'm in because they tried to kill me. I've already done your killing for you. You owe me a straight story. Tell me what it's about, and I'll give you a yes or a no. If it's no, I'll keep your secret, whatever it is, but at least I'll know what direction trouble's liable to be coming from, and I can protect myself.

''Hell, in my line of work, a man who can't keep his mouth shut doesn't last long, and I've lasted long.''

Wardell said, ''What line is that? Gunfighting?''

''I'm a troubleshooter, Wardell. When I see trouble, I shoot it.''

''Not much difference between you and the Treeces after all.''

''I'm still alive.''

''Oh, I wasn't saying anything against you. On the contrary, I've got a feeling that you're just the man for the job.''

''I agree,'' said Manfred.

Wardell turned to the baroness. ''Tell him, Mala.''

Manfred nodded.

''Very well,'' the baroness said, ''I too agree.'' She leaned forward, intent. ''What do you know of Santa Sangre, Mr. Slocum?''

''The old colonial mission, the one that's in the mountains fifty miles west of here?''

''Yes.''

Manfred and Wardell too were leaning toward Slocum, watching him.

''I've never been in the mission, but I've been in Frater, the town that's below it,'' Slocum said.

"And what did you find there?"

"Not much. I was passing through, riding shotgun on a gold wagon. Frater's a mighty unfriendly town." He pronounced it with the A long, so it sounded like "freighter."

"They don't like strangers much," he added.

"Not much," said Wardell.

"Strange country, cut off from the rest of the world. A lot of funny things happen in those mountains. Travelers and prospectors ride in and don't ride out. Sometimes they're found on the back trails with their heads cut off. No heads, just the bodies. Some say there's a tribe of renegade Indians hidden somewhere up on the heights, hostiles who never came in to the reservation.

"Me, I'm not so sure. From what I've heard, Indians think the region is bad medicine and leave it alone. Even the Apache war parties raiding south into Mexico used to steer clear of it. And the Apache don't hardly steer clean of anybody."

"And what do you think, Mr. Slocum?" the baroness said.

"I think that there's somebody who doesn't like outsiders poking around in the back hills outside Frater. Maybe there's a vein of gold there. Maybe somebody just thinks there's gold there, and doesn't want anybody else to find out. The rumor's enough to keep the prospectors coming, but nobody's made a strike there yet.

"Or if they did, they never got alive with it."

"There *is* gold there, Mr. Slocum, a fortune in gold."

Slocum kept from smiling. "Could be."

"You do not believe me, but I tell you it is true. It is not a rumor or legend, but a fact. This I know, Mr. Slocum. I have seen it."

"A lost gold mine?"

"No, a treasure trove. But not in the hills. It's hidden in the mission of Santa Sangre."

8

"You see, Mr. Slocum, I have placed all my cards on the table, as you Americans say."

"Surely not all, Baroness."

"No, not all. The mission is a large place. You could search for years and never find the treasure. If you could, I would not have told you. And it would do no good to try to torture the secret out of the monks, for they do not know it."

"Double-crossing and torture. That's a fine opinion you've got of me."

"You left out murder," Wardell said nastily.

"Murder? Hell, I've done worse than that. I've even been a horse thief," Slocum said, adding in an aside, "but don't let it get around."

"I'm a realist, Mr. Slocum, and I trust you are too, so you needn't play at being offended," said the baroness.

"You know where the treasure is, but you can't get it out by yourself. That's why you need me. That realistic enough for you?"

"So," she said, nodding. "That is true, it is too well guarded."

"Manfred and his boys look capable enough. Where do I come in?"

Manfred said, "My mission is to ensure that the baroness is protected at all times. Her cadre of bodyguards must remain at full strength. Besides, my men are not so expert in this sort of of thing. They are soldiers."

"Not thieves and murderers like me, eh, Captain?"

Manfred looked slightly embarrassed, though not so much that he was running a temperature over it. "You misunderstand me, sir. My men and I are strangers here, outlanders. You know the country, the trails and passes and watering holes. You know the ways of your countrymen, on both sides of the law.

"You see, I speak frankly but not insultingly. Here, you are the expert."

"I'm just trying to find out what you think I can do," Slocum said. "Nobody hires on a gunman unless there's killing to be done. Who is it you want killed?"

"We don't want anyone killed, of course."

"Of course," Slocum echoed, smiling sardonically.

"But the owners of the treasure will hardly stand by and let it be taken away."

"Who're they?"

Manfred fell silent, looking to the baroness to pick up the cue. She said, "Killers—scum—each one a murderer many times over. You need feel no remorse at wiping the lot from the face of the earth. They won't hesitate to do the same time you, as you've already seen."

"The Treeces weren't from Frater, or anywhere near there."

"They were hirelings. Their master comes from Frater."

"And he is?"

"I do not know," the baroness said.

Slocum leaned back, sipping his drink, smiling blandly

over the top of his glass. He was polite enough not to give her a horselaugh.

"The identity of the master is part of the secret of the treasure," the baroness said. "It goes back to the days when Spain ruled Mexico."

"That's a long time ago."

"Longer than you think, Mr. Slocum. It goes back hundreds of years ago, to the first Spanish colony in what is now Mexico City. Among the things that the colonists brought to the New World was the Inquisition, the arm of the Church that finds and punishes heretics. A most potent office once, on this continent and across the sea.

"In the New World, the Inquisition was assisted by the Order of Santa Sangre. A secret society, a military and religious order of warrior monks. In gratitude for their works, the Order was granted great estates in this part of New Mexico. They were required to send a yearly tribute south, and to acknowledge the supremacy of the Church and the king of Spain, but were otherwise given a free hand to run their province as they saw fit.

"They needed slaves to work their great *estancias*, their estates. The mountain Indios were too wild. They did not take to slavery, and died soon after captivity. The Indios of the pueblos, the village dwellers and tillers of the earth, were more tractable. They were enslaved and ruled by the Order with a mailed fist.

"The slaves were commanded to build a great stone church, the church of Santa Sangre. It was part of a mission, a walled compound that was a fortress. Within lay the House of the Order, where its leaders dwelt, ruling the province from their mountain fastness. The province was rich, with exports of gold, silver, copper, salt, corn, and hides.

"The Order squeezed the province dry and kept on squeezing, so that it slid into a long decline. Its holdings had been reduced to the mountain valley where the mission stands when war broke out between Mexico and the United States.

"When the United States became the victor, and moved to occupy these lands, the wealthy landowners of Spanish descent fled south to Mexico, to avoid being despoiled of their goods by the *norteamericano* conquerors. The landowners stripped the churches of their gold and silver ornaments. They then took their own private hoards of precious metals and jewels, loaded them on wagons and mule trains, and fled south.

"The heights of Santa Sangre sat astride two of the principal escape routes, one to the east and one to the west of them. By this time, what was left of the Order had degenerated into a robber band. Now, at the time of the exodus, they came down from their mountain fastness, raiding the wealthy caravans. They killed all they found, men and women and children, that none would be left alive to tell the tale. When the bodies were found, the killings were blamed on the Indios.

"The Order hid their loot in Santa Sangre, but they did not live long to enjoy it. The invading Federal troops, the *yanquis*, discovered their redoubt and laid siege to it. The defenders fought fanatically, but were outmanned and outgunned by the enemy. In the end, only a handful of the Order managed to escape.

"The Federals knew nothing of the treasure. If they had, no doubt they'd still be there, looking for it yet. They tore down the fortress walls and soon moved on, abandoning the ruins.

"Later, when it was safe, the last of the Order returned. They lived in the ruins, alone and forgotten. But there were springs, water wells, which ensured that the mountain valley would thrive again. And so it has.

"In the years since, the town of Frater has grown up

around the ruins. A way station, an oasis in the mountains where travelers may find food and water. But not a friendly place, as you've had occasion to learn at firsthand, Mr. Slocum.''

"Yes, but I never heard of any lost treasure or mysterious Order either, Baroness.''

"You would have, if you had strayed from the trails and roamed the countryside. Or if your gold shipment had been less well guarded. The Order still exists. Who do you think takes the heads of strangers and leaves the bodies for a warning? It is a warning not to pry into their affairs.''

"You don't seem to be frightened off.''

"I am a Rao, of the royal line of the Hyundagari, and not easily frightened. Neither am I reckless or foolhardy. I do not underestimate the enemy. That is why I need your services, Mr. Slocum.

"The Order still guards the treasure. It is not the same as of old. It has kept up with the times. After all, this is the nineteenth century. Frater is a *norteamericano* town, run by men like yourself. Yes, very much like yourself, Mr. Slocum. Ruthless men. Their leaders were recruited long ago into the Order, even unto the second and third generation.

"And the most ruthless are the masters of the band. They alone know where the treasure is hidden, a fact of which the lesser ranks are unaware.''

"*You* know,'' Slocum pointed out. "Are you one of the masters?''

"Hardly,'' she said, smiling with some bitterness. "The Order would rather cease to exist than enroll a woman into its society.''

"Then how do you know the secret?''

"Because I am a woman. But that is of no matter,'' she said, waving a hand in dismissal. "What is important is that not all of the masters are known to me. That is why I do not know who my opponent is. They may be working against me singly or in combination.''

''What about the ones who are known to you?''

''Time enough for them later, when we near Santa Sangre.''

'' 'We'? You're going along too?''

''I know where the treasure is. I am an expert horsewoman and a dead shot, as Manfred will attest. So let's have no nonsense about my being a woman, eh?''

''If you want to risk your neck, that's your business,'' Slocum said. ''Let's talk about *my* business. The way I see it, this treasure is stolen property. It belongs to whoever can keep it.''

''That's how you see it, huh?'' said Wardell, looking up from the bottom of his glass and smiling toothily.

''Yes.''

''That's how we see it too.''

''Where do you fit into this, Wardell?''

He waved his hand airily. ''Consider me an interested party—and a full partner.''

Nobody contradicted him, so Slocum figured that was the way it was. He said, ''Coming along for the ride?''

''All the way, amigo. I'll be right beside you all the time,'' said Wardell.

''Good, that'll give the enemy someone else to shoot at.''

Wardell slapped his holstered gun. ''I can shoot too.''

''In that case, I'd rather have you beside me than behind me.''

''Don't worry. When I kill a man I always look him straight in the eyes.''

''That's a comfort,'' Slocum said. He turned toward the baroness. ''Now, let's talk deal. Who does what, and how much does it pay?''

9

The meeting broke up around ten. Slocum had an urge to get some night air and clear his head, which was spinning with a greedy lust for gold. He went downstairs and started across the lobby. Then the night clerk beckoned to him. Slocum went to the desk. The clerk was the same fellow who'd been working in the day.

He said, "There's a message for you, Mr. Slocum. The sheriff said he'd be over to the Birdcage Saloon."

"Thanks," Slocum said, and went out.

Ten o'clock was late for a weeknight in Los Palos. Most of the buildings were dark, and the few that weren't were islands of light. Slocum turned right when he went out the hotel's front entrance, walking north up the street. He didn't have to ask where the Birdcage was. After spending a few days and nights in town, he knew where everything was. It was a small town.

The row of buildings on the west side of the street was fronted by a wooden plank sidewalk. The boards were warped and sagged in the middle. He walked along the edge of the sidewalk opposite the storefronts. If anyone was lurking in a dark alley, Slocum would have a better chance of seeing them. He'd have walked in the street if not for the horse manure deposited there. He walked light, soft.

The night sky was purple-black, with bright stars and a white crescent moon. The Birdcage was in the middle of the block, the only building with its lights on. It was a two-story wooden-frame structure with a flat roof. The front windows were made up of lots of small square panes set in wooden grids. Light shining through them threw square nets of light and shadow on the street. The windows were dirty, and the light coming through them was a dark smoky yellow. A couple of horses were hitched to the rail out front, their ears pricking and heads turning as Slocum approached.

He went inside, swinging doors rocking behind him. The bartender sat on a stool behind the bar, reading a newspaper. A couple of locals stood leaning against the bar, drinking. Cowhands and ranchers, from the looks of them. A handful of others were scattered throughout the space. Some looked up to see who had entered. When they saw who it was, they looked away in a hurry and went back to whatever it was they were doing.

A roulette wheel stood empty except for a bored croupier, who passed the time by dropping a silver ball in the spinning wheel and waiting for it to come to a stop in a slot, whereupon he'd start the whole process over again.

A couple of "hostesses"—whores—were on duty, walking the floor, trying to get a play. They looked like they'd seen a lot of hard times and bad company and were resigned to a steady diet of more of the same. They perked up when they saw Slocum, not because he looked like he was a stud (sex had stopped meaning anything for them long ago), but because they figured he had money.

He looked around, didn't see Bigelow. A whore arrowed toward him, her painted face like a carnival mask.

"Lookin' for some fun, handsome?"

"I'm looking for Bigelow. He here?"

"He's no fun. Upstairs, the last room to the left of the staircase."

He flipped her a coin, which she plucked out of the air. "Thanks," she said.

"For nothing," she added, when he was out of hearing and climbing the stairs.

On the second-floor landing he turned left, then left again, making a right-angled turn that put him facing the front of the saloon. Below, a haze of smoke hung over the room at balcony height, like a layer of mist over a pool.

At the end of the landing was a closed door. Slocum knocked on it. From inside came, "Yeah, whaddaya want?"

"It's me, Slocum."

"C'mon in."

Slocum entered a corner room, closing the door behind him. Opposite him at a wooden plank table sat Dan Bigelow, facing the door. A double-barreled shotgun stretched across the tabletop, twin bores facing the door, the weapon lying near to Bigelow's hand.

Bigelow took his hand off the stock and wrapped it around a whiskey glass. "Just in time. I thought I was gonna have to drink this all by my lonesome." He indicated a nearly full bottle that stood on the table.

"Taking it kind of slow tonight, Dan?"

"That's my second bottle. Sit down and let me buy you a drink."

"All right," Slocum said. He pulled up a chair and sat down on Bigelow's left, half facing him, half facing the door. He looked around and said, "Nice place."

"It's a dump, but the Birdcage's the only place that's open this time of the night. That's a hell of a note, ain't it? Dodge, Tombstone, Denver, those towns were wide open, roaring at full blast night and day, the saloons never closing."

"They were. They're tamed now."

"At least they're still breathing," Bigelow said. He slid an empty glass across the table to Slocum. "Help yourself."

Slocum did, filling his glass. Bigelow smirked. "Thirsty, huh?"

"All that talking dried out my throat." Slocum took care of that posthaste, draining his glass.

"G'wan, have another," Bigelow urged. Slocum didn't have to be told twice.

Bigelow raised his glass, holding it to the light, studying the amber fluid. "I must make some picture, just another old fart rattling on about 'the good old days.'"

Slocum nursed his drink, silent.

After a few beats, Bigelow lowered his glass and squinted at him. "You could at least contradict me. What the hell, you're drinking my whiskey," he said.

"Oh, I figure that you've got at least one more go-round in you, Dan, even if you are an old fart."

Bigelow's eyes narrowed, glittering. He shoved his face forward, staring up out of his eye sockets. Voice hoarse, rasping, he said, "You got something, don't you?"

"You sure are breathing hard, Dan."

"I knew it!" Bigelow went to pound a fist on the table for emphasis, then thought better of it and rubbed the side of his face instead.

"Must be something big," he said. "What you got, Slocum?"

"You've been making noises like a man itching for some action. You mean it, or are you just sounding off?"

"You've been in this lousy town for a couple of days. I've been here for eighteen months. You're damned right I want action!"

"Even if it goes against the law?"

"Are you serious?"

"That's what I thought," Slocum said. "I could maybe use a partner, somebody to watch my back. There's a lot of tricky angles to this business."

Bigelow was hot-eyed, eager. "What's the game?"

"Robbery."

"Robbery! What kind?"

"Gold and jewels."

"I like the sound of that. Any killing?"

"Plenty, from the looks of things."

Bigelow looked a little more guarded. "You know I ain't squeamish, Slocum, but I'd hate to massacre a bunch of people in cold blood just for money. Unless it's a lot of money."

"It is. Anyway, they'll be trying to kill you, if that makes you feel any better about it."

"Sure. That way it's just business. As long as it's a big payday. How big did you say it is?"

"I'll get to that, but first, there's another important point to keep in mind. There's no law in this. It's a private business. There'll be plenty of hombres trying to kill us, but no lawmen."

"No law, huh? That's a wild one. Now, what could it be? It's a robbery, but whoever's getting hit can't go to the law."

"More of a raid than a robbery, Dan."

"A raid. A raid on somebody who can't go to the law. He can't go to the law because he's outside the law."

"You're gonna steal the loot from a gang of outlaws, is that it?"

"Yes and no," Slocum said. "Ever heard of Santa Sangre?"

"The mission? I've been there. Not to the church, but to Frater. I know the constable there, Jon Basil."

"Friend of yours?"

"Not where gold's concerned. Hell, I barely know the guy," said Bigelow, grinning toothily. "Is that the job, knocking over the Frater bank? Because if it is, the game ain't worth the candle, unless you know something I don't, Slocum. It's a big bank with thick walls and lots of guards, and what's in the vault wouldn't be worth it for the size of the gang you'd need to take it. You'd come out with about a thousand dollars per man tops."

"Not all the gold's in the bank at Frater. . . ."

Slocum told him some, not all, of what he'd heard at the meeting. The level of the bottle had dipped below the half-way mark before he came to a pause.

Bigelow said, "You believe that, about the monks and treasure and all the rest of it?"

"I believe there's gold. And there must be plenty of it, considering what the baroness is willing to pay to take a crack at it."

"Let's see if I got this straight. She knows where there's gold, and she ain't too particular about how she gets it. She's got guns of her own, that whole crowd around here. But she's paying you to get up a gang of your own to steal the gold. Then later, you'll split it up with her, and each go riding off your separate ways with a fortune. That about it?"

"More or less."

"Hell, it's a double cross! She's using you to keep her skirts clean. Soon's you get the gold, you'll get a bullet in the back."

"That's how I figured it. But nobody'd go to that much trouble to set this thing up unless there *was* gold. That's the part of her story I liked."

"I see what you mean. Maybe you got plans of your own, huh?"

Slocum leaned back. "Could be."

Bigelow cracked a broad grin. "That's better. This ain't no charity case you're handing me. This is the real thing. You're gonna need my gun to get that gold, and to cover your back.

"I guess maybe old Dan Bigelow ain't so played out after all."

"I'd like to have you along, Dan."

"Partners? Fifty-fifty share?"

"Partners."

"Now, you're talking!" Bigelow thrust his hand out. "We'll shake on it."

They shook hands. "Hell, we'll drink on it," Bigelow said. He refilled both glasses.

Slocum reached an inside pocket of his vest and fished out a wad of greenbacks. He peeled some bills off the fold and pushed them across the table to Bigelow, repocketing the rest of the wad.

"What's that for?" Bigelow said.

"Wages. I told the baroness that before we could go ahead I'd have to be paid for work done: the Treece brothers. She anted up without kicking. That's your share."

"You killed 'em."

"We're partners now."

Bigelow put the money away. "That's mighty decent of you. I got a confession to make, Slocum. I held out on some of your share of the money I took off the Treeces."

"That's okay. I shaved some of your cut too."

Bigelow barked a laugh. "That's what I like about you. With a fella like you, I know where I stand, ya dirty . . ." He smiled. "Just funning friend."

"Likewise."

Bigelow waved an admonitory finger in front of his face. "What's past is past, but from here on in we share fifty-fifty, right?"

"Absolutely."

They had a drink on it, the two of them looking like a pair of buzzards eyeing each other over a particularly ripe piece of carrion.

Bigelow said, "Where do this Wardell fit in?"

"He's got a say in the thing, but not as much as the woman. I think he's got it bad for her. And the gold doesn't hurt either."

"I heard of him. He's from back East, the black sheep of a rich family that pays him to stay away. He's no powder puff. He killed a couple of gents in gunfights, fair draw, face-to-face."

"He could be a problem," Slocum said.

"So, what's the plan, partner? And how much does it pay?"

"It pays a couple of hundred dollars in advance money, for starters. That's in addition to the money for the Treeces."

"Not bad. I knew I was right throwing in with you. But what's the big payoff? How much's the treasure worth?"

"There's a question. The baroness and company were playing it cagy on that score, but I finally got them to 'fess up that it was worth fifty thousand dollars."

Bigelow pursed his lips in a silent whistle. "Fifty thousand!"

"They said. The funny thing was, I had the feeling they were poor-mouthing me, like they thought I wouldn't believe it if they told me how much it was really worth. Just a feeling I had, but I'm a pretty fair poker player and good at reading faces. From the way they talked, they're counting on this to set them up for life, and fifty thousand minus my cut's not going to be enough for them. They've got expensive tastes."

"How much is your, er, our cut, pardner?"

"I'm in for a third share of the loot. And I figure the

loot's got to be worth at least a hundred thousand. Or more."

"That's a lot of loot."

"I don't think they're too concerned about paying it out. The idea being that I collect in lead, not gold," Slocum said, smiling loosely. After all he'd had to drink, his smile wasn't the only part of him that was loose.

He said, "We're going to need a couple more guns to pull the job. My job is to find them and hire them. They come in for a flat fee: five thousand in gold each, coming out of the treasure."

Bigelow snorted. "I can't see the kind of bad guns we need for the job sitting still for that kind of split once they've seen the treasure."

"The division of spoils should be interesting," Slocum said dryly. "We'll need about three more guns. That makes five, counting you and me. That should be enough for the job.

"I'm hoping you can help me out on that. This is your bailiwick and you know who's around. It'll save time if we can recruit from around here. The ones I know would have to travel, and that takes time. This is a big operation and the faster it moves, the greater chance of success."

"I got a few prospects," Bigelow said. "Let me sleep on it tonight and I'll have some answers for you tomorrow."

Beyond the door, a floorboard creaked faintly. It might have been a noise made by the structure settling, and was not repeated again.

"Well, that's great, just great," Bigelow said too heartily. "It sure was a good day when the wind blew my old saddle pal into town. We sure had some great times in the old days, eh, pal!"

Under his breath, speaking softly so only Slocum could hear it, he mouthed the words, *"Talk it up."*

"It's good to see old friends," Slocum said loudly. "It's good to drink to old friends. It's good to drink, period. Let me pour us another long one, amigo, and then we can reminisce about them there days."

While Slocum kept on rattling along in that vein, Bigelow had silently eased his chair back from the table, standing up and drawing his gun. As Slocum kept talking, Bigelow soft-footed it across the floor to the door, carefully placing one booted foot in front of the other, as if he were walking a tightrope. Any noise he might have made in passing was muffled by Slocum's monologue.

Standing to one side of the door, out of the line of fire if any bullets should come blasting through, Bigelow suddenly yanked the door open.

Into the room fell Virgil, whose sprawling position suggested that he had been squatting outside, listening. He landed on hands and knees, crying out.

With his free hand, Bigelow grabbed the deputy by the back of his neck. Not by the collar, but by the back of his neck, hauling Virgil to his feet with a bone-wrench jerk.

He pressed his gun muzzle against the underside of Virgil's chin, forcing his head back. Virgil's eyes were popping, and his Adam's apple bobbed like a bouncing ball.

Bigelow pulled Virgil's gun from the holster, putting it aside. He growled, "Little pitchers have big ears. What'd you hear, Virgil? Did'ya get an earful?"

"I didn't hear n-nothing!"

"Don't lie to me, you little pissant."

"Honest, Sheriff, I didn't hear nothing, I swear it!"

"If you were more dangerous I'd finish you off right here and now, but you ain't worth killing." He holstered his gun.

"What—what're you going to do?!"

Bigelow smiled evilly. "I told you the next time I caught you snooping I was gonna kick your butt."

He went out the door, hustling Virgil along with him, sweeping him along the railed balconylike landing, turning at the corner, and hauling him to the head of the stairs, with Virgil pleading and babbling all the way.

Bigelow got behind him and planted a mighty kick on Virgil's rump, propelling him into empty space. Virgil howled, arms and legs fluttering, sailing out in an arc that ended below the midpoint of the stairs, where he made contact, bounced, thumped, and tumbled down the rest of the flight, to land in a crashing heap at the bottom of the staircase.

He lay motionless, then moaned, his limbs twitching. The bartender came out from behind the bar and knelt beside Virgil, inspecting the damage for a moment before looking up and announcing, "He's got a broken arm and a couple of busted ribs."

"Too bad it wasn't his damned neck," Bigelow said.

10

That pretty much broke up the party. Virgil lay there, moaning and groaning on the sawdust floor, while somebody went to fetch a doctor.

"Think I'll call it a night," Slocum said, standing beside Bigelow at the top of the stairs.

"If there's one thing I hate, it's a snooper," Bigelow said, mostly to himself. He looked up, glancing at Slocum. "What'd you say?"

"I'm going to head out and get some sleep. Big day tomorrow," Slocum said.

"Yeah . . . yeah!"

"Think hard about those men we need."

"I gotta couple of pips in mind. Two of 'em, no more than a half day's ride from here. They—"

"Tell me in the morning."

"I'll have you up by first light. We can have some breakfast."

"You do that and we're going to have to fight. Maybe you have to get up at the crack of dawn, but I'm going to get me some sleep. From here on in, we're going to be putting in some long hours."

"I can stand it," Bigelow said, "for this kind of payoff."

They went downstairs. When Virgil saw Bigelow standing on the ground floor, he started crawling away from him, whimpering, favoring his damaged right arm and side.

"You better crawl," Bigelow said, "crawl right out of this goddamn town, ya keyhole-peeping weasel."

Slocum said good night and went out. The night air was fresh and clean after the saloon. A man came hurrying into view, rounding the corner of a cross street north of the Birdcage. Slocum's hand snaked to his gun, but before he could draw it, he recognized the man as the town doctor, a compact middle-aged man with twin tufts of hair sticking out of the sides of his head, giving him a lynxlike appearance.

His clothes were in disorder, as if hastily thrown on. The cuffs of a pair of pajama pants were sticking out of the bottoms of his pants. He carried a black medical bag. Seeing Slocum, he veered toward him.

Slocum stood outside the light, but there was enough of a glow shining through the windows and door of the saloon to make his features visible. The doctor slowed his rush when he recognized him.

"Oh—you," he said.

"I didn't do it," said Slocum.

The other glared suspiciously. "Who's killed?"

"Nobody."

"Shot?"

"Nobody. But there's a deputy that's busted up pretty good."

The doctor clapped his hands, rubbing them. "At last! A paying customer," he said, hurrying into the Birdcage.

One of the baroness's bodyguards was sitting in the lobby of the hotel, puffing on a pipe. He studiously avoided looking at Slocum when he entered and climbed the stairs.

On the second floor, the Turk was gone from his post at the far end of the hall, which was now occupied by another of the baroness's men, a slim pale fellow with light blond hair and a well-trimmed silky Vandyked mustache and beard. When Slocum first swung into view, he started, but when he saw who it was he relaxed, easing back into his chair. Slocum guessed that Manfred must have passed the word to the troops that he was *persona grata*.

"I'm one of the club now," Slocum said pleasantly, calling down the hall as he stood in front of his room door, reaching for his key. The guard remained blank-faced, unheeding.

"Well, maybe he doesn't speak the language," Slocum said.

A light shone out from under the bottom of the door. The door was unlocked, the knob turning freely in his hand. Slocum glanced back at the guard, who was stone-faced as before. Slocum frowned, puzzled. He didn't figure the baroness for a double cross, not with all the trouble she had gone to to acquire his services. And it didn't seem likely that any ambushers could have gotten past the guards. Still, he stepped to one side of the door, out of the direct line of fire of anybody in the room. Why take chances?

He toed the door open, nostrils tingling as they were touched by a rich musky scent. A light was burning dimly in the room, but it was bright enough to see by. He peeked around the edge of the door frame.

"Come in," a female voice said throatily. "After all, it's your room."

Once more, Slocum glanced back at the guard, who was pointedly looking up at a corner of the ceiling, minding his own business. Slocum entered the room, closing the door behind him.

He said, "Who's been sleeping in my bed?"

"I'm not sleeping," said Lorelei. She lay sitting up in

bed, her back propped up with pillows piled against the brass headboard, covering herself with a pulled-up blanket. Her neck and the smooth lines of her shoulders were bare.

A pair of high-button shoes lay on the floor, and on a nearby chair lay a pile of garments that included the blue satin dress and some slinky underthings.

"For a second there, I'd thought I'd walked into the wrong room," Slocum said. He tried to keep it light, but got a good look at the curves of her body outlined under the covers, which made his voice thick and choked.

She said, "I kept the bed warm for you."

"That's what I call service!"

She frowned. "I do not understand."

"It's a joke."

"Ah, you make the jest, no?"

"If you don't mind, how'd you get in here?"

"I told the night clerk that I wanted to surprise you. He was a so-nice man and opened the door for me."

"So that's why he was winking at me when I came in. I thought he had something stuck in his eye." Slocum went to the bedside, standing at the head of the bed. "Doesn't look like you've got much on underneath the blankets."

"See for yourself." She let go of the covers so they fell to her waist, baring her above. She was nude, beautifully nude, with full, firm breasts and a delta-shaped torso with a narrow waist and taut, gently rounded tummy. Exposure to the cool air caused her nipples to stiffen, becoming dark brown pebbles ringed by wide, dark aureolas that contrasted with that peculiar tawny skin, which was like a lion's hide sprinkled with gold dust.

She flaunted what she had, and it was worth flaunting. "You like?"

"Sure."

"Come to bed and I'll show you the rest."

"That's mighty sociable of you, ma'am, but this is kind of sudden."

"I like you. Why wait? Life is short, no? And you like me, I can tell."

The way he was standing stiff in his jeans, his attraction to her was obvious. "Isn't the baroness going to miss you?"

"She's gone to bed. Besides, I'm off duty. What I do on my own time is my affair."

He unbuckled his gun belt, slinging it to one side, placing it on the night table where it would be within his reach and out of hers. Not that he expected that kind of a double cross, but one never knew.

He stood at the bedside, looking down at her, his hands hanging at his sides, his mouth dry. She took hold of the top of the covers with both hands, slowly, teasingly pulling them down from her waist, across wide, curving golden hips, down the tops of taut tawny thighs, baring herself to the knees. Her bush was a glossy black-brown thicket, the curls glinting with reddish highlights.

He sank to the bed, covering her, while her arms wrapped around his shoulders, pulling him down to her. Even through his clothes he could feel the heat of her body, and the strength. Under that smooth golden skin lay strong musculature, softened with plenty of yielding flesh at breasts and hips.

Her wide red-lipped mouth opened, her breath moist and steamy-sweet, and he fastened his mouth to hers and kissed her hard. His hands explored her, sliding, caressing, lingering, probing. She plucked at his garments. He broke the clinch long enough to pull off his shirt, tossing it aside. He kicked off his boots and socks and peeled off his jeans, and then he sprang free and erect, naked like her.

He paused long enough to turn down the globe oil lamp burning on the night table, dimming it so that the room was filled with warm golden-brown shadows, which pressed in on the bed, giving just enough light for him to feast his eyes on the beauty of her body.

Then he feasted on the rest of her, licking, kissing, sucking, her legs parting, her innermost sweetness opening to him to meet him, engulfing him in a white-hot ride on a comet. . . .

It had been a long time since he'd had a woman, too long, and the first time he took her fast, and the second time slow, very slow, savoring each deep sensual stroke, and she was there to meet him, matching his eagerness, hunger, with her own, building, stoking the fire, until finally they were writhing on the bed, him holding her succulent ass in both hands as he plowed into her, like hammering nails, and she was throwing it up to meet him, and the tension mounted like a bowstring being pulled tauter and tauter, until—

Release! Flying straight to the targets of desire . . .

Later, they lay awake in the dimness, nestled into each other, her red-haired head pillowed on his arm.

They were making small talk, inconsequential nothings, when out of the blue she said, "Do you like the baroness?"

"I like you," he said, tweaking a nipple that he'd been playfully toying with. It stiffened, and so did he, and one thing led to another. . . .

The darkness was graying, the lamp having been turned out long ago, when Lorelei turned back the covers and got out of bed. Enough light from the outside hall leaked in under and around the edges of the door for her to find her clothes and start putting them on.

Slocum said, "Leaving so soon?"

"Still hungry? Ah, you are insatiable. Don't worry, there will be other times."

"Will there?"

"Can you doubt it? But you must be discreet, very discreet. After all, I have my reputation to consider.''

''It's fine with me.'' When she didn't respond, he explained, ''That's a compliment. It means I like you.''

''So? I notice that you never speak of love.''

''You neither. That's another thing I like about you.''

''We are much alike, you and I.''

''But different where it counts.''

''And *vive la différence*, as the French say, eh?''

''I don't know. I've never been to France.''

''Paris is quite lovely. If all goes according to plan, soon you will have enough money to go where you like, traveling anywhere in the world. . . .''

''Here's hoping.''

''Perhaps you would enjoy the presence of a traveling companion.''

''You?''

''Why not?''

''You never can tell,'' Slocum said. ''Why? You thinking of leaving the baroness's employ?''

''One does not wish to stay in service forever, and milady is not the easiest person in the world,'' Lorelei said. ''But the hour is late and now I must go. We shall talk upon this later, you and I.''

''Talk?'' Slocum said.

''And other things.'' She finished dressing and went to the door, pausing with her hand on the knob.

''The baroness is right,'' she said. ''You are the man for the job.''

She went out. Outside, somewhere in the trees, a few birds chirped. More joined the chorus, while Slocum dropped off to sleep. After that workout, he needed it.

11

"Bigelow! Dan Bigelow!"

Morning shadows still slanted in the streets of Los Palos at a little before ten a.m. as Jerry Jardeen took up a stance outside the jail. Until that moment, there had been lots of citizens out and about, taking advantage of the relative coolness of the morning to go about their business. When Jardeen began shouting his challenge, they started running, taking cover.

"Bigelow, I'm calling you out! Dan Bigelow!"

Jardeen had come to town riding a big white horse, a magnificent stallion. He came alone. He was broad-shouldered, deep-chested, and bowlegged. He wore a flat-brimmed bolero hat with a green snakeskin hatband, a black-and-white piebald vest, a parrot-green bandanna, a white loose-fitting Mexican-style shirt, brown pants, and boots. He wore a brace of Colts, one on each hip, the holsters tied down. A pair of thin black leather gloves, which he had just removed before calling out Bigelow, were folded over the gun belt, held in place against his waist, out of the way of his draw.

He had reddish-gold hair combed straight back with a

widow's peak, and a thick-featured, heavy-lidded, clean-shaven wedge-shaped face. A snake-shaped face. His eyes were dark blue, so dark that they seemed to blend into the black pupils. They held as much warmth as twin gun bores.

His hands were white, soft, pampered. They hovered over his guns.

He had a good pair of lungs. When he shouted, his voice was as ringing brass.

"Bigelow! I'm calling you! You coming out, or are you yellow?! Bigelow, where are you?!"

"Over here, Jardeen!"

Jardeen stood facing the jail, but Bigelow's voice had come from behind him. Jardeen's nerves were good. He didn't move a muscle or betray any surprise.

Bigelow said, "Take your guns out of the holster—slow!—and drop 'em into the street."

Keeping his hands at his sides, well away from the guns, Jardeen started to turn around slowly.

A gunshot sounded, its slug kicking up dirt a few inches away from Jardeen's boots. Jardeen completed the turn.

"You don't hear so good," Bigelow said. "The next one splits ya right down the middle, Jardeen!"

"Better not, Dan," Jardeen said, his voice strong, confident.

Bigelow stood on the northeast corner of the cross street opposite the jail. He held a Winchester rifle at his shoulder, aimed at Jardeen's belly.

He said, "I figured you'd come calling, so I fixed you up a little welcome, Jardeen! I been waiting in the alley here for you to make your play. That fast draw of yours don't mean nothing when I got the drop on you with this rifle.

"Move wrong and I'm gonna kill ya!"

"Aren't you going to give me a fair draw, Dan?"

"Be serious!" Bigelow made a sound that might have

been a laugh, or he might just have been clearing his throat.

"This is the last time I'm gonna tell you, Jardeen! If you wanna live, unbuckle that gun belt real slow and let it drop!"

"Got it all figured, don't you, Dan?"

The sound of the lever jacking another round into the chamber of the rifle was Bigelow's only reply.

Jardeen said, "Better tell him the facts of life, nephew! But don't shoot, not yet!"

"You just say the word, Uncle Jerry," said Dennis Rance, stepping into view from behind the front corner of the jailhouse, leveling a double-barreled shotgun at Bigelow.

"I'll blow the fat bastard out of his boots with his own damned scattergun!" Dennis Rance said.

"Not yet," said Jardeen. "You see, Dan, you're not the only one who knows how to figure the angles."

"Who let the punk out of his cell, my ex-deputy?" Bigelow said.

Jardeen nodded. "Virgil was mighty sore about you busting him up. I showed him how he could get even without risking his own hide, by freeing Dennis from jail. He still had his keys, so all he had to do was slip in the side door while you were out and unlock the boy's cell."

"I'll skin Virgil alive after I've settled with you, Jardeen."

"Want me to let him have it, Uncle Jerry?"

"No!"

"I got my finger on the trigger, Jardeen," Bigelow said. "Even if I take both barrels, you're dead. Bet I live long enough to nail the punk too."

"Bullshit!"

"Shut up, nephew! Looks like we got us a standoff, Dan."

"He's bluffing, Uncle Jerry! I cut loose with both barrels

and the blast will knock him away so he misses you!''

Bigelow said, "He's awful eager to get you killed, Jardeen. That's the trouble with these young gun punks!''

"You called me a punk for the last time, old man!''

"He's working himself up to it, Jardeen. You ain't got long now.''

"Nephew—''

"I can take him, Uncle Jerry! I know it!''

"He's gonna go any second now, Jardeen.''

"Goddamn you, boy,'' Jardeen said.

"It's two to one, Uncle, we can't lose—*ulp!*''

Bigelow and Jardeen had been looking steadily at each other throughout the showdown, neither of them glancing away despite the entry into the scene of Dennis Rance. But that *ulp* that had come from Dennis was impossible to ignore.

Dennis froze, eyes bulging, veins standing out. A foot-long knife was being held at his throat by Slocum, who stood behind him.

"Yesterday when you were boning me during dinner, you asked what this knife was for, remember?'' Slocum spoke pleasantly, almost intimately, into Dennis's ear.

"If you so much as flinch, I'm going to cut your damned head off,'' Slocum said.

The remark was unnecessary, superfluous. Dennis Rance was as paralyzed as a field mouse under the hypnotic eyes of a rattlesnake. He might have been turned to stone, so rigid and unyielding was his flesh.

With his free hand, Slocum reached around the youth, gripping the shotgun by the barrels and tilting it upward, so that it pointed into the air.

"That's a heavy piece for a little runt like you. I better take it out of your hands,'' Slocum said, easing the weapon from Dennis's nerveless grip.

Bigelow said, "I'm glad you didn't sleep in this morning."

"Who can sleep with all this noise going on? I saw what was happening, so I ducked around the back of the jail and came up behind sonny boy here," Slocum said.

"Slocum! I heard you were in town," Jardeen said.

"You heard right."

"What're you doing messing in something that ain't your fight? I've got no quarrel with you."

"You've got no quarrel with Bigelow."

"He laid hands on my nephew and locked him up. Nobody lays hands on my kin without answering to me."

"Want your answer now?" Bigelow said, motioning slightly with the rifle, which had remained trained on Jardeen right from the start.

"Easy, Dan," Slocum said. "Bigelow saved your nephew's hide, Jardeen. The kid was likkered up and trying to pick a fight with me. If Dan hadn't taken care of him, I'd have killed him.

"I might yet," Slocum added, in an aside which only Dennis could hear.

"I didn't know about that, Slocum."

"Would it have made any difference?"

Jardeen shrugged. "Who knows? It's kind of late for second thoughts. The fat's in the fire now."

"Damned right," Bigelow said.

"Maybe not. Nobody has to die," said Slocum.

"No?"

"Think about it, Dan. What we were talking about last night . . . Jardeen's just the kind of man we need."

Bigelow shook his head. "Find somebody else."

"Sure would be a shame to shoot somebody for free when you could get paid for it. That goes for both of you," Slocum said.

Jardeen said, "Sounds like you've got a way out of this."

Bigelow said, "There's two ways out of this. You can unbuckle your gun belt real slow, or you can draw. Which way do you want?"

"There's a third way, Dan," Slocum said. "We can all back off and have a drink and maybe do some business."

"I like *his* way," Jardeen said.

"You would," Bigelow said. "I would too if you had the drop on me, instead of it being the other way around."

Slocum said, "We're all going to have to give a little on this thing, Dan."

"If I let Jardeen out from under the gun, what happens to me?"

"I've got the shotgun," Slocum said. "Listen up, Jardeen. The way things stand now, one word from me and you're a dead man. Dan could drop you before your guns clear the holster, or I could take off your head with the shotgun.

"But I'm taking a chance on letting you get out of this with a whole skin. Why? Because I'm filled with the milk of loving kindness? Because I got religion?

"Hell, no! I'm doing this for one reason only—because there's something in it for me. Now, what do you suppose that might be?"

"Only one thing it could be: money," said Jardeen.

"Uh-huh. What say we have us a little palaver?"

"That rifle pointed at my breadbasket doesn't make me too talkative."

"Put up the rifle, Dan."

"It don't figure, Slocum. I don't trust him."

" 'In God We Trust.' That's what it says on a dollar. I reckon that's one thing we all three can agree on. Dan?"

"Okay," Bigelow said at last gruffly, swinging the rifle barrel to one side of Jardeen.

After a beat, Jardeen grinned.

"Don't make a fool out of me, Jerry, not after all that jawing I just did," Slocum said.

"I'm going to put my gloves on. Okay with you? I'm telling you that so you won't think I'm reaching and get itchy."

Slocum stood with the shotgun braced on his left hip, holding it with his left hand, while his right continued to hold the knife steady at Dennis's taut, throbbing throat. He gave the nod to Jardeen to go ahead. "Nice and easy, Jerry."

Jardeen nodded, pleasant-faced. He pulled his gloves from where they were folded over his gun belt and fitted his right hand into one, flexing the fingers inside it, snugging it, then putting on the other glove.

The gloves would slow his draw, no more than a few fractions of a second perhaps, but it was a gesture of good faith all the same.

Slocum kept the shotgun leveled in Jardeen's general direction, simply as a matter of policy. He took the knife away from Dennis's throat and pushed him forward and away.

Dennis lurched a few steps forward, reeled, buckled at the knees, and fainted, falling in a heap in the street.

"He's okay, he just passed out," Slocum said.

"He must've got it from his daddy, because he sure didn't get it from my sister, his mama," Jardeen said, disgusted.

He went to Dennis, stooped, grabbed him by the collar, and started dragging him toward a nearby horse trough. Dennis came out of his faint before he got there, but Jardeen dumped him in the trough anyway. Dennis sputtered, splashed, and squawked, his head and shoulders festooned with strands of green slime.

"Shut up," Jardeen said.

Dennis fell silent in mid-squawk, his mouth hanging open.

"What about him?" Jardeen said.

"He's Dan's prisoner," said Slocum.

"I sure would appreciate it as a personal favor if you'd let him go. I know he's worthless, but my sister sets a lot of store by him, Lord knows why. I promise you the boy'll keep out of trouble."

"Keep him out of town, I'm sick of looking at him," Bigelow said. "The next time I see him, I'll burn him down on sight."

"Fair enough," Jardeen said. He loomed over Dennis, who lay stuffed into the water trough, arms and legs hanging over the sides.

"You hear that, boy? I gave my word on your good behavior. Go back to the ranch and stay there. If I see you in town I'll shoot you myself, savvy?"

"Y-yes, Uncle Jerry . . ."

"Go on, git!"

Dennis pulled himself out of the trough and stood up, soaked, slimed, dripping, a miserable figure. When he stepped, his boots squelched. After half-a-dozen paces, he looked back, his shoulders hunched, his body quaking.

Through chattering teeth he said, "H-how'm I going to get b-b-back home, Uncle Jerry? I ain't got n-n-no horse."

"Walk."

Dennis started slogging away, moving south, leaving behind a trail of wet boot prints in the dirt.

"Families," Jardeen said, sighing. "Sometimes I wish I was an only child."

"I'd like to get my hands on Virgil," Bigelow said. Slocum said, "He probably hightailed it out of town long ago. Never mind about him, we've got bigger fish to fry."

"You've got my curiosity up," Jardeen said. "What's it all about?"

"I want to hire your gun."

They got out of the sun and went into the jailhouse, where it was cooler. Slocum did most of the talking. He didn't have to say much before Jardeen said, "Okay, I'm in."

He, Bigelow, and Slocum all shook hands and had a drink on it, and then went back to scheming.

12

Wardell said, "A showdown in the streets? Is that what you call keeping a low profile?"

"Call that a showdown? Hell, not a shot was fired," Slocum said. "It was a lot less noisy than killing the Treece brothers, and that came about because of a blunder on your end, friend."

Before Wardell could reply, Manfred said quickly, "That's what worries me. I've been unable to get any leads on who might have told them about Mr. Slocum."

It was noon in the dining room of the Dorado Hotel, on the first floor rear. The room had high ceilings, a brown tile floor, and sets of French doors opening on to a patio. A couple of the baroness's bodyguards stood watch on the patio.

The baroness and her party occupied a table in a corner of the room, a location that Slocum noted was out of the line of fire of any snipers who might try to take a potshot from outside.

The table was set with fine white linen, china plates, and heavy silverware. Seated there were the baroness, Lorelei, Manfred, and Wardell. Seated nearby at a small round table was the Turk, who ate nothing and scowled at everyone, including the waiters who moved around the baroness's group, serving the various courses.

The baroness wore a thin lightweight toast-colored riding jacket and long brown skirt. Lorelei was more casually dressed, in an embroidered white sleeveless blouse and dark fringed skirt. Manfred wore an expensive casual suit that would have looked at home on a Continental *boulevardier* gentleman, while Wardell's blue pinstripe suit would not have been out of place back East in a boardroom meeting. What would have been out of place was his string tie, the cowboy boots worn under his pants, and the Western-style gun belt buckled around his waist.

Slocum had sought out the baroness to bring her up to date on his further plans, and had found her lunching with her entourage in the dining room. She had invited him to join them at table, so he had pulled up a chair and sat down. He hadn't been seated for more than ten seconds before Wardell had started boning him about the Bigelow-Jardeen showdown that had taken place earlier.

Slocum had settled that, and now was ready to move on to other business. The baroness said, "Perhaps you would care to have something to eat with us?"

"I'm sure Slocum's got plenty of other things to occupy his time," said Wardell.

"Not at all," Slocum said. "It's too danged hot to be out in the sun anyhow, and besides, I'm starving."

The waiter was signaled, and set another place for Slocum. On the table were serving bowls of salads and fruit, platters of cold meat, roast beef, chicken, and the like, loaves of sliced fresh bread, rolls, dishes of salsa and sauces, and so on.

When the waiter had finished serving him, Slocum stared at his plate for so long that the baroness was moved to inquire, "Is something wrong with your food, Mr. Slocum?"

"I don't know. I'm still trying to find it," he said. "You call this a portion, waiter?"

"Er, pardon me, sir?" the waiter said, puzzled, mildly apprehensive.

"What're you trying to do, starve me to death? What you laid out on my plate is barely enough to choke a fly. Never mind, I'll just help myself to some more," Slocum said, and did, heaping his plate high with the good things.

"What's that you're drinking, Baroness, wine?"

"Why yes, Mr. Slocum. Would you care for some?"

"Don't mind if I do." He saw the waiter starting for the wine carafe, and said, "I'll handle the honors, friend. You're a mite too stingy for my liking."

The carafe was at the other end of the table, but Slocum had a long reach, one that would have served him well at the most crowded boardinghouse table. He filled his wineglass to the brim.

"*Saludos,*" he said, lifting the glass. When he set it down again, it was empty. He fixed that—he refilled it.

"I see the vintage meets with your approval," Wardell said through a sneer.

"Very refreshing," Slocum said.

He picked up his knife and fork and dug into his plate.

"You are a man with a healthy appetite, Mr. Slocum," the baroness said dryly.

"Ummmm," Lorelei purred, prompting the baroness to look at her with raised eyebrows.

Someone was playing with Slocum's foot under the table. Lorelei, he guessed. It was a pretty sure bet that it wasn't Wardell. Slocum glanced up from his plate, not interrupting the steady flow of food that he shoveled into his mouth. His expression was bland, mild.

Lorelei winked at him out of the corner of her eye, while

the foot that was rubbing against his moved higher up his leg.

Finally, he rested his fork on the edge of a now-clean plate, saying, "Whew!"

Wardell said, "Now that you've finished stuffing your face, maybe you're ready to tell us your plans."

"Who's finished? I'm just taking a breather before having seconds," Slocum said. "Besides, I never talk business while I'm eating. It's bad for the digestion."

Not until coffee had been poured in thin china cups and dessert sampled did Slocum lean back in his chair and begin to discuss the matter at hand.

"Bigelow and Jardeen have come in with me," he said.

"Bigelow? The sheriff? Why, he's a fat old man!"

"Try saying that to his face, Wardell. Just try. He's an old-timer, all right—an old pro. He's cleaned up more tough towns than you've ever been in.

"And Jardeen's a good man. That is, he's a bad man, but he's good for this kind of ruckus. Him and Bigelow are each worth a half-dozen ordinary guns."

The baroness nodded. "I have confidence in your judgment, Mr. Slocum. After all, that is one of the reasons why you were hired."

"When the sun's lower, the three of us are going to take a ride south to Meseta, a town a couple of hours away from here. It's a pretty rowdy place, with plenty of bad hombres looking to hire out their guns. I should be able to fill out the rest of my team there.

"Also, there's plenty of horse traders, so I should be able to pick up a string of horses there for a decent price. There's always lots of dealing going on, horses being sold across both sides of the border, so my tradings shouldn't attract any attention," Slocum said.

"Excellent," the baroness said. "Will you be returning to Los Palos?"

"Not if I don't have to. Once I've got the men and the horses, it'd be better to make straight for the rendezvous outside Santa Sangre. Speed counts on a raid like this."

"Unquestionably," Manfred said, nodding vigorously.

"So, with your permission, I'll be on my way," Slocum said, pushing his chair back from the table. There wasn't much left to eat anyway.

The baroness nodded. Slocum rose. Manfred said, "You will be leaving now for Meseta?"

"Hell, no," Slocum said. "Ride in the hot sun, after eating a big meal like this? It'd ruin me. No, I'm going to take a siesta, then head out in mid-afternoon when it's cooler."

He pulled on his hat, touching the brim. "See you."

He crossed the dining room floor, passing the Turk. He nodded at him, smiling with his lips. The Turk stared straight ahead, not acknowledging Slocum with so much as a blink.

Slocum shrugged, exiting.

13

It was an hour or two before sunset when Slocum, Bigelow, and Jardeen rode out of the hills into the town of Meseta. The hills were low and rounded and dark brown, as if burnt. A river ran out of them, narrow, shallow, and greenish-brown, slowly winding its way across the flat in long lazy S-curves. The river was bordered on both sides by bright green vegetation. The ground was yellow-brown.

The town lay near the banks of the river, a couple of handfuls of whitewashed adobe cubes that were houses and buildings. There was a plaza and an old Mission-style church. Checkerboarding the outskirts were green squares that were irrigated fields.

The road into town was a length of gritty yellow-white dirt that tasted flinty in Slocum's nose and the back of his throat when he breathed in the dust kicked up by his horse's hooves. He and the other two riders and their mounts were powdered with a layer of trail dust from taking the long hot hard ride from Los Palos.

It felt good to pass through the cool blocks of shadow cast by the first houses at the edge of town. The dirt trail became a cobblestoned road hemmed in on both sides by bright white walls.

Nary a soul was in sight.

"Where is everybody?" Bigelow said.

Slocum shrugged. Jardeen said, "Maybe they're taking a siesta, or working in the fields."

"It's too late for a siesta, and I didn't see anybody in the fields, did you?" Bigelow said.

"Come to think of it, no," said Jardeen. "Reckon some-one's laying for us?"

Slocum shook his head. "I think not, but you never can tell."

It was a small town, and it didn't take them long to get to the center of it, as the crooked cobbled lane spilled into the plaza. It too was deserted, except for an old beggar woman who sat in the shadows of the church, on the front steps.

The riders passed close by her. She looked like a sun-dried mummy wrapped in a black shroud. She sat with her legs crossed and her back to the wall, holding a begging bowl in her lap. In it were a few copper coins. Her withered hands were like gnarled roots.

As the riders drew abreast, she lifted up her head, turning her face toward them. Her eye sockets were black hollow holes, liked cored dried apples.

"Blind," Bigelow muttered.

Jardeen peeled the glove off his right hand, fished a silver dollar out of his pocket, and flipped it through the air. It fell into the brass begging bowl with a *clink*.

The beggar woman snatched it up and made it disappear, mumbling something that might have been thanks.

"Ask her if she knows where everybody is," Bigelow said.

Jardeen said, "I don't think she savvies too good."

"You'd be surprised, these old gals know plenty."

"Are you speaking from personal experience or what?"

"Don't try to make something dirty out of it, Jardeen. Just ask her."

"I don't think that was English she was speaking, and I don't speak much Spanish."

"I do," Slocum said.

"So you ask her," Bigelow said.

Slocum had leaned over the side of his horse, toward the woman, opening his mouth, when a series of crackling noises went popping off in the near distance.

"Gunfire," Bigelow said.

"Well, now we know where everybody is," Slocum said. "Nice to know it's not aimed at us."

Jardeen said, "If you want *pistoleros*, go where the shooting is."

The noises came from somewhere on the far side of town. From here, they sounded like a string of firecrackers going off.

"Maybe it's a fiesta," Jardeen said.

"I don't hear no music, no brass bands," Bigelow said.

They crossed the plaza, entering a zigzagging street, threading it until it gave on an open space outside town. A crowd was gathered there, men, women, and children. Most of them were *campesinos*, local small farmers and their families.

They didn't look happy. They had grim, stolid faces, even the kids. They threw some dirty looks and low mutterings at the three newcomers as they came riding into the scene.

The crowd was massed on a flat-topped ridge, a good stone's throw away from the edge. Between them and the edge stood a gang of armed men, a dozen or so, toting rifles and six-guns. Perched along the rim of the ridge, hunkering behind rocks and bushes, were a couple of riflemen, occasionally sniping shots down into the hollow below, shooting at an unseen target. It was the sound of their shooting that Slocum and company had heard in the plaza.

The trio reined in and dismounted, swinging down from the saddle. ''Looks like this is as far as we go,'' Bigelow said.

Except for the snipers, the rest of the gunmen stood out of the line of fire of whoever was down in the hollow. Not that any shots had been fired from that direction since Slocum had arrived.

The gunmen strutted and stalked around self-importantly. Half were Anglo cowboys and half were *vaqueros*, but they all were commanded by the man in the center of the band, a white-haired man with a clean-shaven pink face and a pair of round-lensed spectacles. He looked more like an accountant than anything else, except for his cowboy hat, holstered gun, and knee-high riding boots. Even with the high-crowned hat he was short, but he bawled out orders like a crowing rooster.

Bigelow stood with arms folded across his chest, unimpressed. ''Buncha cowpokes with six-shooters, that's all.''

''Slim pickings,'' Jardeen agreed.

A flatbed wagon rolled up, pulled by two horses in tandem, and driven by another of the gun-toting cowboys. The wagon was reined in to a halt. Then some of the other gunmen unhitched the team and led them away. All the while, the bantamweight bawler was in the center of things, giving orders and directing the action.

The rear gate of the wagon was lowered, and the gunmen began loading rocks into the bed, heavy rocks to weight it down.

''Wonder what they've got in mind?'' Jardeen said.

Another gap opened in the surly crowd of onlookers, and through it came a small two-wheeled cart being drawn by a long-eared jackass mule. The back of the cart held a couple of stacked wooden crates. There was no driver, but a lone man trudged on foot beside the mule, holding it by the head harness.

The cart handler was a strange duck, round-shouldered and bandy-legged. He wore a frayed top hat and a shabby bottle-green checked coat that would have looked right at home on the back of a drummer in St. Louis. He was a long way from St. Louis. He had long thick straw-colored hair falling in strands to his jawline, which resembled that of a bony fish. His pale eyes were set close together, with a turnip nose between them.

The crowd gave him a wide berth, opening on both sides to put some distance between them and him, as if he were the bearer of a contagious, and potentially fatal, disease.

Even the bantam and his bravoes didn't want to get too near to the mournful green-coated apparition.

Bigelow pushed his hat back, then scratched his head. "That little asshole looks familiar, but I just can't place him."

"That's Doc Primus," Slocum said.

"Who?"

"Doc Primus. He's a dynamiter."

Jardeen said, "That's what it says on those crates of his: 'dynamite.' No wonder everybody's giving him so much elbowroom."

"Maybe we should too," Bigelow said.

Slocum said, "Doc's a pretty good blast man, from what I recall. Leastways, he's still got all his fingers and toes. I met him a couple of years back in the Rockies, when he was blasting a tunnel out of the side of a mountain for the railroad.

"Basically, he walks the line, but from what I hear, he's been known to blow open a safe or two if the money's right."

"We could use a man like that," said Jardeen.

"Think I'll mosey over and have a little chat with him,

say how-do-you-do,'' Slocum said. ''You two stay here.

''No, on second thought, maybe you'd better move back some, just in case.''

Bigelow said, ''In case of what?'' But Slocum had already started walking toward Primus. Bigelow was left standing holding the reins of his horse and Slocum's. He and Jardeen exchanged glances, Jardeen shrugging. The two of them started drifting away from the area, walking the horses.

The donkey cart had rolled to a halt near the big wagon. Primus threw the handbrake and secured the reins. He signaled to the white-haired man, who had been keeping his distance. Not very happily, the white-haired man went to him—not too near.

He put a hand beside his mouth, calling, ''What do you want, Primus?''

''I need a couple of hands to unload the crates and help me load them on the wagon, Mr. Holloway.''

''Coming right up.'' Holloway turned, walking quickly in the opposite direction, toward a knot of his men. He ordered two of them to go help Primus. They went, not liking it much.

The helpers got to work. The first crate of dynamite was set aside, placed carefully on the ground by the duo, who handled it as gingerly as if it had been a crate of eggs.

''Don't worry, those sticks of dynamite are harmless,'' Primus said.

''Harmless,'' one of the helpers repeated, grimacing. His partner rolled his eyes, looking skyward.

''They can't go off by themselves, not until I attach the blasting caps. Now, these here caps are dangerous, fluky things. It doesn't take much to make them go off,'' Primus said, smiling at their discomfort with a mouthful of crooked yellow teeth.

The helpers lugged a crate of dynamite to the wagon,

loading it into the hopper. While they were putting it down, one of the snipers on the rim fired a couple of shots down into the hollow, causing both men to start.

Doc Primus took a chaw of tobacco, wedging it between his jaws and grinding it to a pulp. It gave him a lift while working, and smoking was definitely not recommended around all those explosives.

He pried open the crate on the ground, which was filled to the brim with bundles of dynamite. He set to work with the blasting caps, primers, fuses, and lengths of detonating cords. From time to time he let fly with a spurt of tobacco juice.

The helpers finished loading the last of the crates into the wagon. One said, "You need us for anything else?"

"Just to pick up the pieces later," Primus said.

One of the two started moving away, but the first, the one who had spoken, delayed his exit when he saw a long-legged stranger loping easily toward the dynamiter.

He moved to intercept the newcomer, saying, "Keep back, mister. This's a private party."

"I'm a friend of Doc's here," Slocum said. "Hey, Doc!"

Primus looked up from where he sat squatting on his haunches, using a pocketknife to cut a length of fuse cord. "Who's that? Is that you, Slocum?"

"Sure is, Doc. Long time no see." Slocum turned to the gunman who was blocking his way, saying, "I kind of help Doc out on his little operations. Unless maybe you'd rather, if working with tetchy explosives doesn't bother you?"

"Hell, no! It's yours and welcome to it," the other said. He moved off, going in the direction his partner had taken, rejoining the main body of men grouped in orbit around Holloway.

Slocum hunkered down beside Primus, who kept on un-interruptedly rigging the dynamite.

"What brings you down this way, Slocum?"

"I might as well ask you the same question, Doc."

"Oh, the usual. Trying to make a buck. It's been slim pickings since the Southern Pacific job was wrapped up. Can you believe it? Only a couple of months ago I had a highly skilled and well-paid job working for the railroad, and now I'm reduced to picking up pocket change by wandering from ranch to ranch, blowing up boulders and tree stumps."

"Life is funny. Didn't you save that good railroad pay?"

"Sure, I saved it—for whiskey, women, and the gambling tables. It was the tables that really skinned me. But just you wait, as soon as I get some working capital, I've got a system that'll bust the bank of those gambling halls. I'll get even, you'll see!"

"Seems to me you had a foolproof system for winning the last time I saw you, Doc."

"This one is better," Primus said shortly.

"What're you doing here, blowing up tree stumps? Must be a big one, to judge from all the dynamite you've got."

"You might say I'm cracking a hard nut, Slocum. See that spry little fellow over there, the one with the white hair?"

"Yes. I heard him too. He sure does a lot of crowing for a rooster with so few pinfeathers."

"He's got a lot to crow about—say, would you mind handing me that bundle of cord over by you? Thanks.

"Anyway, that's Old Joe Holloway, one of the biggest ranchers in these parts. I'm working for him."

"Doing what?"

"Down in the hollow there's a hardcase holed up in a farmhouse. Name of Aldo Tambrel. Maybe you've heard of him?"

"Red-hot Mexican *pistolero*, wears a shoulder-holster rig?"

"The same."

"He's supposed to be good."

Primus nodded. "Just how good may be seen by the half-dozen or so dead Holloway men scattered around the bowl. But don't try to see for yourself—stick that head of yours over the rim for a peek, and like as not Aldo'll shoot it clean off."

"What's the beef between him and Holloway, Doc?"

"Aldo was in a cantina last night and got into a scrape with one of Holloway's riders over a girl. Aldo gunned him, and Holloway's men decided to teach him a lesson.

"So far the learning's been kind of one-sided. Aldo killed two more of Holloway's men last night, and put another three out of action. He was making his break when he had his horse shot out from under him. He managed to make it to the farmhouse down there with a rifle and a couple of bandoliers filled with bullets.

"The house was abandoned, but it's still in pretty good shape, with thick adobe walls and a clear field of fire all the way up to the rim. And Aldo is a dead shot with a pistol or a rifle. The house is on a tongue of land that sticks out into the river, so it's surrounded on three sides by water. Nobody's coming for him that way. The only way to come at him is straight down the hill, into the hollow. That's what the dead men tried."

"How many in Aldo's gang?"

Primus looked up from his cutting and splicing, surprised into laughter. "Gang? What gang? It's just Aldo. Of course, he's kind of a one-man gang."

Slocum said, "One man's holding off this whole outfit?"

"Yes, and doing a pretty good job of it. You've got to admire him, in a way."

"You admire him so much that you're planning to blow him to kingdom come."

Primus shrugged. "Funny thing, Slocum, but blowing up

people pays a hell of a lot better than blasting tree stumps out of the north forty.''

''Ain't it the truth?''

''Holloway's getting nervous. He figures that if Aldo holds out until sundown, and the way he's going there's no reason why he shouldn't, that come the darkness he might be able to make a break. And Mr. Holloway is none too easy about the thought of Aldo's getting away loose, able to pick the time and place to settle the score.''

Slocum nodded. ''From what I hear, Aldo's not the forgiving kind.''

''Holloway neither. He knew I was in the area doing odd blasting jobs, so he sent for me. The idea being that I roll a wagonload of dynamite down the hill into Aldo's lap, and boom! No more farmhouse, and no more Aldo.''

Stretched out on the dry grass in front of Primus were a number of bundles of sticks of dynamite, with each bundle having an individual fuse that was spliced into a main trunk line of cord. When the end of the main line was lit, the cord would burn down to touch off the many individual fuses branching off from it, touching off all the bundles more or less simultaneously.

Primus glanced over his shoulder at his patron, who was pacing back and forth, glaring impatiently from behind round spectacle lenses.

''His nibs is getting antsy,'' Slocum said.

''If he doesn't like it, he can do the rest himself. This is one job that can't be rushed. Almost done, though . . .

''I'd like to sit here for a while longer and make him fume, just on principle, but the shadows are getting long and the light's closing fast, so I'd better get the show going.''

''Okay, Doc, I'll drift. I don't want to distract you. Afterward, maybe we can have a drink.''

''Why not?''

"You'll be flush with cash, so I'll let you do the buying."

"Holloway's not paying me that much. He's a cheap so-and-so, so tight he squeaks. I mention that in case you're thinking of hiring on with him."

"Furthest thing from my mind."

"He's going to need some men. Aldo opened up a lot of vacancies in his outfit," said Primus. He gathered up some bundles of dynamite and rose. "Being around all these explosives doesn't make you nervous in the least, does it, Slocum?"

"If you're not bothered, why should I be?"

"Ah, but I'm a professional, this is my trade."

"I've handled dynamite before, Doc. Not like you, but enough to know that being scared around it's the surest way to get yourself blown sky-high."

"True, true."

"Of course, you're a wizard with it, Doc. It's a pleasure to watch you work. So I'm going to stand back and do just that.

"See you later," Slocum said.

He turned, angling across the ridgetop to where Bigelow and Jardeen now stood by the horses. Primus climbed into the back of the wagon, and began attaching the bundled sticks of dynamite to the various crates, each of which were filled with dynamite.

When the fuse was lit, each individual bundle would in turn detonate the crate to which it was attached, thus triggering a big blast all at once.

Primus clambered over the crates, adjusting fuse-cord lengths, periodically letting hawk with brownish streams of tobacco juice that fell dribbling on the weeds.

Slocum joined Jardeen and Bigelow. Jardeen said, "What's up?" Slocum told them what he had heard from Primus.

"That Aldo's got a lot of sand, making a stand like that," said Jardeen.

Bigelow said, scoffing, "What's he gonna do? If he gives up, he either gets a bullet or a neck-stretching at the end of a rope. At least this way he gets to go out with a blast."

"Maybe not," Slocum said.

"He will if your boy Primus is as good as you say he is."

"He is, but that's not what I meant."

Jardeen said, "Sounds like you've got an idea, Slocum."

"That's what's worrying me," said Bigelow.

Slocum told them what he had in mind. Jardeen was thoughtful. Bigelow frowned, his furrowed forehead looking like a swatch of corduroy.

"I don't like it," he said. "It don't figure. What's the percentage in it?"

"We could use Aldo," Slocum said.

"There's plenty of good guns in this neck of the woods."

Slocum made a show of looking over Holloway's men. "Not up here . . . present company excepted."

"So we'll go someplace else."

"Aldo knows all the crooks on both sides of the border. He could get us a good deal on some horses."

"We can get them someplace else too."

"It all takes time, and we've got a rendezvous to keep."

"It don't figure," Bigelow stubbornly repeated. "Why stick out our necks if we don't have to?"

"Aw, it's not that much of a risk, not with these galoots. It'll be fun."

At this, Jardeen broke into a slow smile. Dreamily he said, "It *would* be fun. . . ."

"I can see I'm outvoted," Bigelow said. He threw his hands up in disgust, saying, "What the hell, it'll be fun! Oh, sure, in that case let's do it! If I say no, then I'm the dog in the manger, the old dog who can't run with the pack!

"The hell with that. I'll show you who can cut the mustard, assholes! So, you wanna have some fun, huh?"

Bigelow reached for his gun. Slocum easily put his hand on top of Bigelow's, so the gun couldn't be unholstered.

"Easy, Dan. Don't jump the gun, so to speak," Slocum said.

A couple of men on the edges of Holloway's group had noticed the minor commotion, and were looking hard at the three strangers. Bigelow caught the play and nodded, suddenly beaming, all smiles. Slocum and Jardeen were all smiles too. Slocum took his hand off the other's gun hand, and pretended to brush a speck of lint off Bigelow's shoulder.

Jardeen laughed and clapped his arms on the back of the others' necks, in a gesture that said they were all pals. The laughter and gesture looked phony as hell, and did nothing to lessen the suspicions of Holloway's men.

A couple of them put their heads together and started talking, occasionally glancing up at the strangers.

At that moment, Holloway began bawling a fresh round of commands, and his men, all of them, hopped to what he was saying, their growing misgivings about the strangers forgotten in their haste to suck up to the boss.

The blast-wagon was ready to roll. The plan was for the men to push the wagon near to the rim, yet still far away enough to be out of Aldo's line of fire. Another advantage they had was that the man in the farmhouse was unaware of what was being planned for him, since the infernal machine had been built where he couldn't see it. The first he would know of it would be when it came rolling down the slope of the ridge, barreling toward him on a collision course with the farmhouse.

Before that happened, it would be necessary for the fuse to be lit. Primus had timed it so that there would be enough fuse cord to keep on burning during the time it would take for the men to push the wagon the rest of the way over the rim and while it was descending, so it would explode within seconds of having crashed into the farmhouse.

Holloway's men were none too keen about standing around the wagon after the fuse had been lit—or before it, for that matter. Eight or nine of them were grouped in a loose arc around the wagon, while Primus and Holloway stood to one side, Primus briefing the rancher on the fine points and last-minute details.

The snipers on the rim kept up a steady fusillade, firing down at the farmhouse to keep Aldo pinned and to hide the noise of the blast-wagon in the crackling of gunfire.

Slocum turned to the nearest group of locals and said something to them in Spanish. Their faces, at first indifferently sullen, became masks of astonishment. They turned and fled, shouting warnings to their compadres, who on hearing, also broke into a run.

He'd told them to take cover. Bigelow and Jardeen had already moved farther back with the horses. Slocum raised his rifle to his shoulder and pointed it at the wagon.

He hoped Primus was far enough out of the way. To be sure, he blasted a slug into the ground near Primus's feet.

There was plenty of firing going on from the snipers shooting into the hollow, so the single rifle shot hardly stood out. Except for Primus. He jumped back, saw who was shooting, and started running, abruptly dashing away from Holloway, leaving him in mid-sentence.

Holloway, astonished, caught sight of the puff of smoke from Slocum's weapon, and grabbed for his own six-gun.

His men, gathered around the wagon, saw the crowd of onlookers suddenly break and scatter in the opposite direction. Some of the gunmen started to run too. Others hauled their guns clear of their holsters.

Holloway's gun was leveled, but it was too late, because

Slocum had already swung the rifle to cover one of the clumps of dynamite clinging to the top of a crate and was squeezing the trigger for his second shot.

He put a bullet in the middle of the bundle, exploding it. The blast triggered off a far greater blast in the crate, which set off the next crate, and so on, setting off a series of ever-greater explosions that erupted like a volcano blowing its top.

For an instant, the wagon—and the men around it—were outlined in shadows at the heart of a red-white-yellow inferno. A fan of light and heat sliced upward, a wedge of hellfire slanting into the sky. Shadow-wagon and shadow-men ceased to exist, vaporized.

Force and pressure waves hammered sky and earth, racing outward like circles expanding from a very big rock dropped into a very small pond.

The multi-blasts unleashed roaring cataracts of noise, storm, and smoke. All was chaos.

14

Swirling clouds of smoke, reeking of sulphur and cordite, hid the scene. It was as if a vent of Hell had opened on the hilltop.

Stuff fell from above, pelting the earth with debris, scraps of wood, and flecks of flesh.

Wind blew, tearing at the clouds. A few minutes later, the veil of murk had lifted, though a haze hung over the surroundings.

A smoking crater now gaped where the wagon had stood. Scattered around it were scarecrows that were men, strewn about the raw, gouged earth.

Slocum, Bigelow, and Jardeen moved across the ground, guns in hand, walking in a wide, loosely ranked line. Slocum was in the middle, flanked by Jardeen on the left and Bigelow on the right.

Jardeen held a gun in each hand, at waist-level. On his left, way over on the rim, motion stirred. A sniper who lay sprawling facedown suddenly raised himself up, lifting a rifle from the ground.

Jardeen pointed a gun at him and fired, dropping the man with a slug in the forehead. He shot with seeming casualness, almost offhandedly, dropping his man as if poleaxed.

A handful of Holloway's men who hadn't been manning the wagon were stunned but alive. There was no fight left in them. It was an easy matter for the three to round them up and disarm them.

Slocum said, "You two watch these. I'm going to look for Primus."

"I can hear you, you don't have to shout," Bigelow said.

"I can't hear so good myself, my ears are ringing." Slocum trudged off in the direction where he had last seen Primus before the blast. He stepped past a waist-high boulder. On the other side of it was a man, one of Holloway's men. He sat with his back against the rock, his head down and his legs sticking straight out. In one hand he held a gun, which was resting in his lap. He was blackened and scorched by the blast.

He was as surprised to see Slocum stride past as Slocum was to see him. The man's eyes were very white in his blackened face. They widened, then narrowed, glancing at the gun in his lap.

"Don't," Slocum said.

The man brought his gun up. Slocum's gun was already in place. He fired. The man stiffened against the rock, then went limp, the gun slipping from his dead hand.

Slocum kept walking, not breaking stride. A few paces ahead stood a clump of small shrublike trees, crooked and dwarfish. Behind them was a bathtub-sized dry basin lined with a cluster of prickly pear cactus.

Nestled on the bed of thorns was Primus. He lay on his back, like an overturned turtle, his arms and legs waving feebly. His hat was gone, his clothes were black and tattered, and his hair was singed.

Slocum used his free hand to haul Primus out of the basin, and helped him to his feet. He kept his gun in hand, not pointing it at Primus, just keeping it ready for any sudden surprises that might develop.

Primus was dazed, his eyes foggy. His mouth and chin and front were stained with glistening reddish-brown stains, not blood but tobacco juice. Primus broke into a coughing fit.

When he came out of it, wheezing, he said, "W-what happened? The last thing I remember, I was running, then something lifted me up and threw me into the air—after that, things go blank."

"The wagon blew up ahead of schedule. One of Holloway's men must have touched it off by mistake or something," Slocum said.

Primus's eyes shifted into focus and lost some of their glassiness. His face set in scowling lines.

"Slocum! Now I remember—*you* were shooting! You're the one who set it off!" Primus grabbed Slocum's shirtfront in both hands. "Why'd you do it, you loco son of a—*ulp*!"

Slocum had stuck the tip of his pistol into one of Primus's nostrils, bringing his outburst to an abrupt halt. Primus froze.

"Take it easy, little man. You're still dizzy from the blast and obviously not in your right mind, or you wouldn't have taken hold of my shirt the way you're doing.

"Because if you were in your right mind, then I'd just purely have to kill you for laying hands on me, savvy?"

Primus opened his fists, releasing the folds of fabric that had been bunched up under his fingers. Carefully, he smoothed them out, patting them back into place against Slocum's chest. Then and only then did he take a step back, the pistol's muzzle coming free from his nostril with an audible *pop*.

He put the back of his hand against his forehead, pressing it there with a gesture he'd cribbed from the heroine of a stage melodrama he'd seen in St. Louis.

"Sorry, Slocum, I guess I'm still out of my head, don't know what got into me, heh, heh, heh. . . ."

"Sure, that's what I figured," Slocum said, his face and voice radiating sincere concern. "A fellow can't take that kind of pounding without his brains getting scrambled some.

"You feel better now?"

"Much better. Much much better. I came to my senses right when you stuck that gun in my nose. Yes, sir, that sure was effective, like a dash of cold water in the face."

"Glad to help out." Slocum eyed the other appraisingly, from head to toe. "You don't look too bad. A little the worse for wear maybe, but no bones broken."

"No . . ."

"So cheer up, things could be worse."

Primus couldn't hold his irritation. "You could at least have waited until after I'd gotten paid! Holloway wouldn't fork over a nickel until the job was done!"

"Don't worry, I'll see that you don't lose by it, Doc."

Primus opened his mouth to say something, realized what Slocum had said, closed his mouth, then said in sweet, cooing tones, "You will? Well, er, that's mighty decent of you, big fellow, mighty decent! I might have known that you wouldn't leave an old friend forlorn and penniless through no fault of his own!"

"That's what friends are for, Doc. Hell, didn't I risk my own neck by firing a warning shot to tip you off?"

"Did you? I mean, why, yes, you did. Of course. You never did anything without a good reason, Slocum. Still," he said, his voice becoming rueful, "you might have let me in on the plan."

"It was a kind of spur-of-the-moment thing, Doc."

"But there is a plan, right? This is all part of some greater scheme, isn't it? Tell me that it is."

"It sure is. A real moneymaker," Slocum said.

"Excellent, excellent. Tell me, what became of my erstwhile employer Old Joe Holloway?"

Slocum shrugged, looking around. "Maybe that's him over there," he said, pointing to a figure that lay between the boulder and the prickly pear patch, about a dozen paces closer to the edge of the ridge.

He and Primus went to it, Slocum holding Primus above the elbow, steering him and supporting him.

"By Jove, it is him!" Primus said.

Holloway lay flat on his back, stiff, arms sticking out from his sides, legs spread. His glasses still clung to his face, twisted at crazy angles, the left lens webbed with spidery cracks.

His clawlike hands were empty, as was his holster.

"He doesn't look so big now, in death," Primus said. "Of course, he didn't look so big in life either. He was a very little man."

"He hated big enough," Slocum said.

"Still, where is he now? Wherever he is, you put him there."

"I can stand it."

Primus went to his knees beside Holloway, and began searching him, turning his pockets inside out. He lifted the flap of his jacket and reached deep into an inside breast pocket, his face lighting up as his fingers encountered Holloway's billfold. He drew it out into the open, and found a fat wad of greenbacks.

He said, "Looks like I get paid after all—*awk*!"

Holloway came to spitting, snarling life, grabbing Primus's wrists, clawing at the folded greenbacks. In a deep, strong voice, he cried, "Give me back my money, you crook!"

Primus fell back, breaking the other's grip while still holding onto the money. He scrambled to his feet, saying, "Ah-hah, so he's not dead after all!"

Holloway jumped up, readying himself to pounce on Primus. Slocum waved the gun under Holloway's nose, but Holloway ignored it. Less easy to ignore was the ungentle tap with the gun barrel that Slocum laid across the side of his head.

Holloway crouched, cursing, nursing his torn scalp and bloody ear, glaring up out of hollow eye sockets at Slocum, the busted left lens of his glasses giving him a particularly demented aspect.

He said, "You're a pretty big man with that gun, damn you!"

"Uh-huh," Slocum said.

"If you had an ounce of balls, you'd give me a gun and have it out in a fair fight!"

"Like the kind you gave Aldo?"

"He's a vicious outlaw who only deserves to be shot down like the mad dog he is!"

"Funny, that's what some of the townsfolk were saying about you."

Wary caution came into Holloway's good eye, the one behind the clear lens. "You a friend of his? You, a white man, siding with a Mex against your own kind? Why, damn your eyes—"

Slocum wagged the gun barrel over toward where Bigelow and Jardeen had herded what was left of Holloway's gunmen into a miserable huddled knot.

"We'll go over there, so your men can tell you what a great job you're doing," Slocum said.

"Give me a gun and I'll shoot your guts out!"

"Mosey."

Holloway staggered, lurching stiff-legged. Slocum marched him over to the others, with Primus in tow.

Jardeen said sleepily, "Is that your dynamiter?"

"That's him."

"He looks like he was shot out of a cannon."

Holloway limped over to his men, none of whom could look him in the eye. The contempt on his face was scathing, scalding.

"A fine bunch you are! You're about as useful as teats on a boar hog, you no-shooting pack of puking milksops," he began.

A soft sound of a few rocks falling somewhere beneath the rim was the only forewarning of the arrival of a newcomer, as a man suddenly popped into view as he scrambled up the side of the ridge, hopping onto the top.

He was medium-sized, compactly knit. He had short dark hair closely cropped to the scalp, cordovan-colored skin, thick bushy eyebrows, wide dark eyes, and a well-trimmed black beard. He wore a long-sleeved loose-fitting white peasant's shirt, a pair of black bell-bottom pants, and elaborately hand-tooled fine leather boots. His gun belt was worn in a unique style, draped over his shoulders so the holster hung butt-out under his left arm. A couple of bandoliers of ammunition were looped over his right shoulder. In both hands he cradled a well-worn Winchester, which was leveled at Slocum and company.

Slocum, Jardeen, and Bigelow had both the prisoners and the newcomer covered by guns.

Slocum said, "Welcome to the party, Aldo."

"Señor Tambrel to you, gringo."

"Tsk-tsk. Is that any way to talk to the man who saved your life?"

"Who are you?"

"Your guardian angel."

"Save the fairy tales for the priests and children, amigo. How are you called?"

"The name's Slocum."

Aldo nodded, as if that explained things. "I have heard of this Slocum. Seven, eight years ago, at the crossing at Blood River in Texas?"

"That was me."

"So. Some hombres from my home village died there. Killed by you maybe?"

"Maybe. They shouldn't have been out slave-hunting for women."

Aldo waved the rifle barrel negligently, as if in dismissal. It never wavered more than an inch or two off target, and that target was Slocum.

"No matter. They were all pigs, like these ones," Aldo said, indicating Holloway's men. "I heard a noise, so I climbed the hill to see what I could see.

"But what is it I see?"

"They had a wagonload of dynamite for you."

"And?"

"I made a big noise, and you see the rest," Slocum said.

Aldo held the rifle in one hand, gripping it at the top of the stock, his finger resting on the guard a hairbreadth from the trigger. With his other hand he stroked his chin.

He thought it over for a while, and when he stopped thinking he cracked a big grin, revealing a gold upper front tooth.

"You can call me Aldo, amigo," he said. "And Holloway? What became of him?"

"You're looking at him. This little wizened runt," Slocum said, indicating Holloway.

"That's him?"

"Don't you know what he looks like?"

Aldo shook his head. "I never met him. I could hear him shouting orders up on the hill, but he never showed himself where I could take a shot at him.

"So this is the so-*grande* Señor Holloway, eh? *Jose Viejo*. Old Joe. He sounded bigger. From the voice, I thought he would look more like *him*," said Aldo, indicating Bigelow.

"He looks like a lawman, that one," he added.

"He's an amigo too," Slocum said.

"He does not look very friendly."

"I'll be damned if I go around with a simpering grin just to get on your good side, Tambrel," said Bigelow.

"A lawman, *sí*," Aldo said, nodding. "And this one," he said, indicating Jardeen, "this one looks like a *pistolero*."

"Like you," Jardeen said.

Aldo didn't deny it. "But this one, the one you say is the *jefe*, the chief, this so-Old Joe, you know what he looks like?

"A dead man."

Holloway turned to Slocum. "You're not going to let this greaser shoot me down in cold blood?!"

"Give him a gun," Slocum said.

Jardeen nudged Bigelow. "Give him your gun."

"Give him *your* gun. You got two."

"Nobody but me handles these guns."

"The same goes for me, friend."

A couple of guns that had been taken from the prisoners lay piled against a tree stump. Slocum took one, checking to make sure it was loaded. He came up behind Holloway, pressing his own gun barrel against the back of the rancher's skull.

"Hands up and no tricks," Slocum said. He dropped the gun in Holloway's empty holster. He stepped back and to the side of him, still covering him.

Aldo set his rifle butt-first on the ground, leaning it against a boulder so that it stood upright. He stood facing Holloway, with less than five paces between them.

He crossed his hands over his chest, nodding. "Any time . . ."

Holloway clawed for his gun. Aldo whipped the pistol out of its underarm holster and fired before Holloway's gun had cleared leather.

The gunshot sounded tinny compared to the dynamite blast earlier. The slug tagged Holloway in the middle, rocking him backward. Aldo advanced, arm straight, gun held out in front of him, firing.

Holloway sat down hard, then fell back, flat. He lay face-up, sunlight turning the lenses of his glasses opaque, glinting. His mouth gaped. After a pause, blood trickled from the corner, dribbling down his chin.

Smoke curled from the barrel of Aldo's gun, sending wisps crawling up past his face as he stood over Holloway, looking down. Sunlight sparkled off his gold-toothed grin.

"*Gracias*, amigo. But why do you do this thing for me?"

"I've got a job for you," Slocum said.

.15

The abandoned mine lay southwest of Santa Sangre, in a region of long parks and high plains separated by rugged mountain ranges. Slocum and company reached the site in early evening, two days before the scheduled rendezvous with the baroness's group.

There was Slocum, Bigelow, Jardeen, Tambrel, and Doc Primus, all on horseback. They came through a mountain pass in single file, trailed by a string of horses, enough for a spare mount for each of the men, plus a few extras. The horses served as pack animals, laden with supplies: food, water, weapons, ammunition, and explosives.

The band broke out of the high, narrow rock-walled pass, into the open oval of a flat piece of ground. The site had been scouted earlier by Slocum and Bigelow, who had gone on ahead to make sure that it was untenanted by friend or foe.

The oval was about a half mile long on its long axis, and a quarter mile across at its widest point. It was hemmed in on all sides by cliffs and peaks, but the apparent solidity of those rock walls was deceptive. They were honeycombed with passes, trails, culverts, and canyons.

The rocks were black, brown, gray, and red, eroded by sun, wind, and time into twisted fantastic shapes. The oval flat was yellow-brown ground, overgrown with dry weeds, barrel and prickly-pear cactus, and yucca and aloe plants.

In the northeast face of a cliff there was a gaping hole, roughly the size and shape of a railroad tunnel. Indeed, a set of narrow-gauge railway tracks emerged from the tunnel mouth, stretching to the middle of the flat. The line had once been used for ore cars to ferry crushed mineral-bearing rocks out of the depths of the mine.

Now, the rails were rusted and warped, and in some places had broken free of the timber ties, sticking up in the air like twists of licorice. Scattered about on the ground were overturned ore carts, their wheeled trucks rusting and weed-grown.

In the center of the site, where a cluster of buildings had stood, all that remained were fire-blackened foundations.

Wind blew through the passes, making lonesome wailing cries. The sun was still up, but had gone behind a mountain, throwing the flat into purple shadow.

Horses and men were dusty and fatigued as they entered the scene, hoofbeats pounding on cracked, sunbaked ground.

Aldo said, "I have wronged you, large one. Out here on the back trails, you no longer look like a lawman."

"Yeah? What do I look like?" Bigelow said.

"A *bandido*."

Jardeen said, "Lawman, bandit, what's the difference?"

"The wrong side of the law pays better," Bigelow said.

"You should know," Jardeen said.

"You're damned right I do."

Doc Primus sagged in the saddle, clinging with both hands to the saddlehorn. "Whew! I'm played out. You damned near killed us, Slocum, prodding us so hard to get here."

"A little healthy exercise won't kill you, Doc."

"Won't kill *you* maybe. I'm no trailsman, I don't even like the outdoors. And speaking of trails, you must've picked the roughest, most broken ground in the territory for us to travel."

"Dan picked the route, not me. But it worked. Nobody was waiting for us on this trail. Hell, I don't think anybody else even knows about this trail."

Bigelow said, "Back about ten years ago, when the mine was working, I used to ride shotgun on some payroll deliveries to the miners. I got to know the lay of the land pretty good in them days. You had to, to stay ahead of the outlaws."

Primus said, "What I want to know is, what's the all-fired hurry? The rendezvous isn't until the day after tomorrow."

"But I want to go to the rendezvous site tomorrow for a look-see, to make sure there won't be any surprises," Slocum said.

Aldo said, "Where will we make camp?"

Jardeen pointed at the tunnel mouth. "How about over there? We'll have a roof over our heads and our backs covered so no one can sneak up on us from behind."

"Forget it," Bigelow said. "It's filled with bats."

"So what? I'm not afraid of a few bats," Jardeen replied.

"How about a few thousand of them, five or ten thousand bats?"

"Quit your joshing. The tunnel's not big enough to hold that many bats."

"Oh, yeah? This area, under these mountains, is honeycombed with limestone caves. Networks of 'em, some stretching for miles underground. When they were working the mine, they broke through into one of those caves. A big limestone room, bigger than a church. Half the bats in creation must've been hanging from the ceiling. They'd get in and out from some smaller caves high on the cliffs, until the tunnel was built. Now they use that for the front door. That's one of the reasons the mine was closed. That, and the vein of ore playing out around the same time.

"See that white stuff lining the tunnel, and the rocks and ground outside? That's batshit. Wait'll the sun goes down and you'll see the whole crowd of them come out. It's something to see," Bigelow said.

"We must be batshit to come here in the first place," Primus said.

"Lots of snakes around too," Jardeen said. "They're making the horses skittish."

"They're making *me* skittish," said Primus.

A few score snakes were sunning themselves on the flat rocks in the center of the site. The riders steered well clear of them, making for a cliff on the southeast side of the oval. A tilted overhang jutting from the base of the rock face provided some shade, and there was sweet grass for the horses to graze on.

There they pitched camp. Primus stepped down stiffly from the saddle and walked around bowlegged and hunched forward, a hand pressed to the small of his back.

"I think I busted my tailbone," he said, moaning.

"I'm gonna kick it up around your ears if I catch you shirking your share of the work, like you been doing since we hit the trail," Bigelow said.

"I'm not used to manual labor."

"That's for damned sure."

Primus held up his hands. "If I should lose my touch or my hands should shake when I'm rigging the explosives, we could all be blown sky-high."

"That don't mean you can't help unload the horses same as everybody else," said Bigelow.

Aldo took a rifle and a pair of field glasses, and climbed to a high point that would serve as a lookout. Below, the others made camp. Horses were freed of packs and saddles, fed, watered, and groomed. The needs of the horses came first. A man left on foot in this country was a man in trouble.

A rocky spur projected from the cliff base like a scorpion's claw, providing natural shelter for the campsite. A section of it was roped off to serve as a makeshift corral, penning the horses. They were also hobbled for the night.

Slocum called up to Aldo, manning the sentry post. "See anything?"

Aldo shook his head, then went back to scanning the broken hills.

Jardeen said, "Think we can risk a fire?"

"I reckon so," Slocum said.

"Good, a hot meal will go down nice. I'm sick of all that jerked beef we had to eat on the trail."

Soon there was a campfire going and food sizzling over the flames. A thin line of smoke rose into the sky, which was fading from blue to white. The oval flat was now completely encompassed by deepening purple shadows. A breeze stirred up a sweet scent of sagebrush.

A crescent moon hung in the space between two peaks, brightening in the darkling air. A handful of stars shone palely at the top of the sky.

On earth, shadows went from purple to black, overflowing the nooks and crannies that held them, covering the land in a web of darkness. The shadow lines looked like cracks in the earth's crust. They thickened, swelling, meeting their neighbors to form large planes of blackness. The planes grew, squeezing out the fading patches of light.

A block of shadow fell across the tunnel mouth, creeping over it until it was engulfed by inky black.

From somewhere inside the tunnel came a stir of motion, sounding like tree boughs shaken by the wind. The sound grew, becoming like the fluttering of flags in a high wind, many flags. It grew so loud that the famished men looked up from their meals, forgetting even to chew in the mounting intensity of the moment.

Suddenly a black mass vomited out of the tunnel mouth, exploding up and out into the open air.

It was a whirlwind, a cyclone of countless thousands of what looked like tattered black scraps of fabric or paper whipping around in a circular column, spiraling higher and higher into the sky.

Like the genie freed from the bottle in the fables of old, the horde of bats poured out of the tunnel by the hundreds, the thousands, swirling around in a vortex, whipping up the air with their multitudinous wings.

Soaring aloft, they flew up out of the oval, above the rock walls hemming it in. When they were high enough, they peeled outward and away, scattering to the four winds in search of the night's prey.

It was very silent when they were gone, except for the nickering and pawing of the ground by the unnerved horses. Blazing firewood crackled and popped.

"Damn," Jardeen said softly. "I didn't know there were that many bats in all the world!"

"Told ya," said Bigelow, smug.

Primus said, "Tomorrow night we find another campsite!"

Slocum said, "Tomorrow night we'll be at the rendezvous. And the night after that—Santa Sangre."

"Amen, brother," said Primus.

16

There was death and the smell of burning.

It was early in the morning, only a few hours past dawn. The sun was behind the mountains in the east, leaving the village of Three Forks still wrapped in blue shadows, with dew on the grass. A stream emerged from the hills, winding across the flat south of town.

It was a place where three trails met: a trail that ran north to Frater mountain valley; a trail from the east, through mountain passes down to the plains, and from there to Los Palos; and the thin and twisty canyon trail from the southwest, eventually meeting the old mining site. The canyon trail was lost and almost forgotten, its mouth choked by dry brush in the Three Forks vicinity.

A village had taken root there, thanks to its location at the junction of the passes, and its freshwater stream. It wasn't much of a place, just a collection of ramshackle buildings housing a trading post/feed store, a blacksmith shop, a stable, a combination assaying office and post office, and a handful of private dwellings, mostly one-room wooden cabins.

Now, it had been uprooted, the buildings burned, the

inhabitants massacred. Bodies lay sprawled in the open, covered with masses of carrion-eating birds. Men, women, and children. Slocum was still a fair distance away from the scene, but he was close enough to see that.

What was left of the buildings were mounds of rubble and charred timbers. The fires had long since gone out, but the smell of burning clung to the valley, blanketing it in a smoky haze.

The destroyers had left sentries. Two of them stood on the heights overlooking the eastern approach, watching for signs of movement. It did not escape Slocum that that was the way he and his men would have been most likely to take. That was why he hadn't taken it, instead detouring south and west to the old mines, so he could enter the Three Forks valley from behind. It hadn't hurt to come a day early either.

He and the others had gotten up earlier today, while the sky was still black. They'd eaten breakfast, broken camp, saddled up, and been ready to move out before first light. The bats were returning to the tunnel, not in one great mass as they had done when leaving it, but steadily filtering in, wheeling and fluttering and flying into the great round black hole in the rocks.

The gang had hidden some supplies, burying waterskins and cartons of food in the arid ground, then piling a cairn of rocks on top of the cache to prevent wild animals from digging it up.

As the sky grayed, they moved out, riding into a canyon on the east side of the oval, a steep rocky gorge whose hairpin twists and turns would eventually lead to Three Forks. That was what Bigelow said. The others had to take his word for it since none of them knew the territory, and the trail wasn't shown on any of the sketchily detailed maps of the region.

The trail certainly seemed to have been forgotten by the

rest of the world. Its sandy floor was marked only with the tracks of coyotes, deer, and smaller varmints. In some places the gorge was so narrow that the riders could only travel in single file. Throughout the trek they scouted ahead, making sure that what lay behind the next blind corner was all clear. The rock walls of the gorge rose up and up, not quite meeting at the summit, but leaving a narrow strip of sky.

Jardeen said, "You couldn't get a wagon through here."

"That's what the extra horses are for," Slocum said. "They brought supplies in, and they'll bring gold out."

"Those foreign dudes might have something to say about that."

"We'll have to make them see reason."

"Sure." Jardeen grinned, the laugh lines not reaching his eyes.

The gorge opened up, widening, letting more light in. It was still gray and shadowy, like being at the bottom of a shallow pool.

"We're almost there," Bigelow said. "Another quarter mile or so of twists and turns, and the trail ends."

They halted on the far side of the last blind curve before the trail mouth. Slocum and Aldo went ahead, on foot, rifles in hand.

The canyon mouth was blocked by a mass of dead trees and dry brush that had been piled up there. The horses wouldn't be able to get past it, but it wouldn't take much work to clear the obstruction.

Aldo slung the rifle by a strap across his back, and began scaling the rocks on the left-hand side of the gorge. The rock face looked sheer, but he seemed to have no trouble finding handholds and footholds, mounting the cliff like a lizard climbing straight up the side of a wall. About a third of the way up, he reached a ledge that angled up and around the limb of the rock. From that vantage point, he had all of the Three Forks valley laid out below him.

He climbed back down and told Slocum what he had seen: death.

Aldo raced back along the trail to warn the others. Slocum crept up to the gorge mouth, using the brush wall for cover. He eased himself into the spaces where the edge of the brush barely met the cliff. There was a space in the thicket, a hollow that managed to fit him if he sat with folded legs on the sand. He parted the bushes enough to give himself a peephole on the valley.

He saw burned buildings, bodies, buzzards. He saw the two sentries on the far side of the valley, manning their lookout posts above the eastern approach. Their horses were hitched to a tree at the base of a pinnacle. Apart from them and the birds, he saw no other movement in the valley, no signs of life.

More than once in the past, Slocum had fought those ultimate desert warriors, the Apache. He had come out of it with a whole skin, no mean feat, considering. He and Aldo were the best outdoorsmen of the gang, so that meant they would deal with the sentries.

They slipped out of the gorge, low-crawling into rocky cover, where dozens of boulders littered a slope that dipped into the valley. Bigelow and Jardeen crouched at opposite ends of the bush wall, rifles at the ready to supply covering fire if needed. Primus stayed back behind the bend, holding the horses and serving as a rear guard.

Slocum and Aldo made their way down the slope, dodging from rock to rock, flitting across open spaces in the span of a few heartbeats, showing themselves as little as possible. Their passage was as noiseless as a hawk's shadow gliding across the land.

They worked their way down to the stream, where there were waist-high rushes and green grass and trees. A few bodies sprawled facedown in the open between the stream and the village, fugitives who'd been shot down while try-ing to escape. Not all of them were males, or all adults either.

The stream wound east, clear across to the other side of the valley. The woods lining its banks were a green-canopied pathway for Slocum and Aldo.

Slocum was less worried about being seen by the sentries than he was about blundering into a large group of mounted men. He figured that it had taken a fairly large-sized group to have massacred the village. It didn't seem they were still around, but if they were, he wouldn't care to be pinned down by them while on foot. Or any other way.

The sun had edged the cliff tops by the time Slocum and Aldo had worked their way to the east wall. Horizontal sunbeams shafted across the top of the valley, turning the tips of the western peaks into molten gold.

In the middle of the eastern wall there was a hundred-yard gap, a notch that opened on a wide boulder-strewn slope cut by the trail switchbacking up from the far-distant flatlands.

One sentry manned the cliff top north of the gap, while the other manned the post on the south. Slocum pointed to the one on the north, then pointed to himself. Aldo got the idea, nodding. Slocum put a finger across his lips, signaling the need for silence. Aldo raised a sleeve, baring his left forearm. Strapped to it in a slim leather sheath secured by thongs was a flat black throwing knife. Aldo grinned, show-ing his gold tooth.

They split up, Aldo melting into the rocks at the base of the south cliff, Slocum moving north. Slocum had to make a wide detour to avoid the too-open space in the neighbor-hood of the notch. By the time he reached the north wall, sunlight had burned the dew off the grass.

Even in the shadows at the bottom of the cliff, it was

hot. Slocum was sweating. This sure was a lot harder work than just putting a bullet into somebody. . . .

A couple of hundred feet north of the gap, on the inside wall, there was a cleft in the rock the size of a high-steepled church. A narrow trail corkscrewed its way along the inside of the cleft to the cliff top.

At the foot of the cleft there was a grove of pine trees with shaggy blue-green boughs. The scent of the pines was fresh and clean in Slocum's nostrils.

There was also the smell of horses and manure. The sentries' horses were tethered in the grove. Slocum moved downwind of them, so as not to spook them with his strange man-scent. He didn't know it, but he was radiating murder from every pore.

He eased through the pines, stepping into the grove just as he became aware of yet another smell, the aroma of tobacco smoke.

It came from the fat black cigar being puffed by a man who was sitting on a fallen tree in the grove. He was a stocky man, with a high balding forehead, bushy eyebrows, and wide side-whiskers. He wore a hat with a rounded crown and a flat brim, like a preacher's hat. He wore two guns, and a rifle stood leaning against the fallen log beside him.

He sat there puffing, trying to blow smoke rings. He was so absorbed in what he was doing that he didn't notice Slocum until he was almost on him, bearing down on him with long swift strides and an eighteen-inch Green River knife in hand.

The smoker's mouth fell open, the cigar dropping out. He lunged for his rifle, grabbing it as Slocum's backhanded slash took him across the throat, cutting it.

The man tried to scream, but could manage only a choking gurgle. That too was cut short as Slocum thrust the knife into his chest, the point sliding over the top of the rib cage and entering the heart, stopping it with instant death.

Slocum grabbed the rifle so it wouldn't fall. The dead man slumped into a heap in front of the fallen log. His hat fell off, rolling on its brim like a wheel for a few paces.

Slocum ground out the lit cigar with a boot heel. He could use a smoke himself—he wanted one so badly he could taste it. It would kill the smell of blood and other stenches.

He glanced up at the cliff top, where the sentry stood with his back turned, looking east, unaware of what had happened a couple of hundred feet below. The bulk of the cliff blocked the view of the sentry on the south wall, if he had even been looking in this direction.

Slocum gripped the corpse's wrists and dragged the body under the pine trees, out of sight. The hat was still lying in the middle of the grove, and he went back to get it.

The horses pricked their ears and stamped the ground, but were undisturbed by the bloodshed and death. Maybe they were used to it, like warhorses unaffected by the sights and smells of slaughter.

Slocum entered the cleft in the rocks and started up the long winding trail to the top. The overhang at the summit hid the cliff top from view. He couldn't see the sentry, but the sentry couldn't see him either. And the recessed cleft was set back and in shadow, screening him from the sight of those who might be roaming the valley floor.

The trail was steep and narrow, in some places little more than a game trail, with dizzying emptiness yawning just beyond the edge of the footpath.

Slocum padded upward, gun at the ready. If anybody spotted him he was going to start shooting, and the hell with keeping quiet. But nobody did, and he reached the top.

He peeked over the rim. The summit was covered with

thin sandy soil and small stunted trees. The sentry was
about a dozen yards away, sitting on a round rock with the
rifle across his lap.

Slocum could see across the gap, to the south wall. The
sentry there suddenly lurched forward, back bowing as if
struck from behind. He staggered stiff-legged, reaching behind his back to claw at something. He fell facedown. What
looked like a handle stuck between his shoulder blades was
Aldo's throwing knife. Aldo was nowhere in view.

The north-wall sentry jumped up, dashing to the edge of
the cliff, stopping about ten feet short of it. He peered
across the way, trying to see what had happened.

Slocum came up behind him and knifed him in the back,
then shoved him off the cliff. It was a long way down, and
the body hit with a crunching thud.

Aldo popped into view on the opposite cliff top, waving.
Slocum waved back.

17

Slocum found Manfred in the graveyard.

The graveyard sat on top of a small knoll west of the village. The burial ground was barely bigger than a cabbage patch. There was no fence, no gates. Crosses stuck out of the weedy earth at odd angles. Most were wooden, but there were a few made of wrought iron. There were no headstones.

Manfred sat on the ground, leaning back against a cross near an open grave. His chin rested on his chest and his eyes were closed. He looked like he was unconscious or dead. He was in bad shape. His clothes were tattered and filthy. The front of his shirt was discovered by a melon-sized dried bloodstain. His face was drawn, taut with suffering and pale from loss of blood. His hands were open and empty, with no sign of a weapon.

Slocum went to him, a rifle in one hand and a drawn gun in the other. Earlier, on the cliff top, he'd spotted the figure in the graveyard and thought he'd seen it move, although it had remained stone-still for the rest of the time he'd watched. He'd descended to the ground, where he and Aldo had dragged the body of the dead sentry off to the side, dumping it out of sight under some bushes. They'd gone to the horses in the grove. He and Aldo had both had enough of being on foot. Let the horses do the walking. Slocum had mounted up on a roan mare, while Aldo had chosen a chestnut stallion. They'd agreed that Slocum would investigate the graveyard, while Aldo fetched the rest of the gang. Aldo had taken the third horse in tow, riding off to the western trail mouth, while Slocum had headed toward the graveyard. Reaching the knoll, he'd dismounted, hitched the horse to a tree branch, and gone the rest of the way on foot.

Flies buzzed around Manfred. His eyelids flickered at the sound of grit scuffing under Slocum's boot soles as he approached. Manfred's eyes opened. They were filmed, feverish, the light behind them dimming but not yet out. It took them a moment before they focused on the intruder, brightening slightly when he recognized Slocum.

Slocum hunkered down beside him. "Manfred . . ."

"Mr. Slocum . . . so they did not get you. That is good."

"What happened?"

"My throat is very dry . . . do you have some water?"

Slocum didn't have a canteen with him. "I can get some—"

"No! Don't go . . . by the time you return, I will be dead. . . ."

"You're not so bad off."

Manfred's lips quirked at the corners in what might have been a smile. "I have said the same thing to too many dying men on too many battlefields to be fooled by it myself. My time is almost done, but I must tell you what happened here. . . .

"We rode into a trap. . . . They were already in the village, waiting for us. . . . They knew . . . *he* knew, that cunning devil. . . . We were caught in a cross fire, my men and I . . . never had a chance.

"He proved to be a better commander than I, may his soul rot in Hell. . . ."

"Who?"

"The baron."

"The baron?!"

Now Manfred was smiling, a bitter smile. "You see, Mr. Slocum, where there is a baroness, there must also be a baron. Nikolai Zoloff, the baron.

"He has no royal blood. He's a commoner with pretensions to nobility. He gained the title when he married the baroness. She is of the royal bloodline, not him. . . .

"When he married her, he also became Master of the Order of Santa Sangre, by right of the law of succession."

"Zoloff's the Master?"

"Yes, Mr. Slocum. As the baroness said, the rules of the Order prevent a woman from holding power, so the office goes to her consort. But Zoloff and the baroness had a falling-out. She was a constant reminder of his ignoble origins.

"Before he could do away with her, she fled. Those of us who were loyal to the rightful heir gathered around her. We planned to kill Zoloff and his followers and take the treasure, but we could not do it alone."

"And that's where I came in," Slocum said.

"Quite so. Unfortunately, we had not reckoned on Zoloff's power, his network of spies and traitors. His agents sent word to him that we planned to assemble here, and he was ready for us.

"My men were shot down like dogs. I too was shot. My foot caught in the stirrup as I fell, and I was dragged away when my horse ran. My foot worked free and I fell near here, away from the battle. I still have enough vanity left that I would not care to have you think that I fled from the fight!"

"I never would've thought that, Captain."

"Later, when the shooting was done, they came looking for me. I hid in this open grave, thinking it would indeed be my grave, and I passed out. . . . When I awoke, it was morning, and I climbed out of the grave . . . not for long, I know.

"I should be dead now. I didn't know why I somehow kept on living, but now I do. . . . It was so I could enlighten you."

"What about the treasure, Manfred? Is it real, or was all that part of the come-on?"

"It is real . . . real gold, jewels, a chest of it."

Sweat broke out on Slocum's forehead. "Where is it?"

"I do not know."

Slocum felt as if a cold stone had just hit the pit of his stomach.

"The baroness knows," Manfred said. "If you want the gold, you'll have to save her. They have her."

"Where? In Santa Sangre?"

"At the mission, yes. But be quick. She will not live long, if Zoloff has his way. . . .

"A most amusing jest, is it not, Mr. Slocum? To get the gold you must first save the baroness. And with your lust for gold, I think it shall not be long before I am revenged on Nikolai Zoloff. . . .

"And so, I die happy."

Manfred slumped forward, his eyes open. The light behind them was gone. Slocum touched his neck, feeling for a pulse. There was none. He was dead.

Slocum closed Manfred's eyes. Before he could raise up, he heard hoofbeats, lots of them.

The knoll was overgrown with bush, shrubs, and weeds, screening him from view while he was squatting down beside Manfred. Screening Manfred from view too. That was how the old soldier had managed to escape detection after the massacre. Slocum had seen him only because he was looking down from above, on the cliff top. The sentry had been focused on the east, and had missed Manfred.

Slocum couldn't be seen from ground level, and yet the hoofbeats were fast closing in on the knoll. They came from the north, not the south, so it couldn't be the rest of his gang.

How did the strangers know he was here? With a groan, Slocum remembered the horse he had tethered at the base of the knoll, in plain view. They had seen the horse, and were coming to investigate. Maybe they had noticed that the sentries were missing too.

But that didn't mean that he had been seen, not yet. . . .

He drew his gun and put it in Manfred's dead hand, resting it across the top of his thigh so it could clearly be seen. Then he hopped into the open grave, ducking down.

It was a shallow grave, about four feet deep. No doubt it had been intended to be filled by a recently deceased villager, before the general slaughter had wiped out the entire population, such as it was.

The inside of the grave smelled of damp earth. Slocum heard horses and riders reining in at the knoll.

"There he is!" somebody shouted.

Another cried, "Look out, he's got a gun!"

Gunfire exploded. Slugs whizzed by overhead as Slocum crouched in the grave. The bullets tore into Manfred's body, knocking it down from where it was sitting with its back to the cross.

The shooting continued, sounding like a firing squad. Somebody shouted over the racket, "Hold your fire!"

The shooting died down. "We got him!" somebody crowed.

The shooting stopped. The gunmen were on the east side of the knoll. Some climbed to the top and pushed their way through the weeds, making for the graveyard.

"Look! It's old Manfred hisself!"

"He's got the shit shot out of him."

"The baron's going to be mighty glad about this!"

Slocum peeked over the top of the grave. Four men were coming in a loose line, smoking guns in hand. They were laughing, joking, clearly unaware of any lurking threat.

Behind them, two more stood on the slope of the knoll, holding the reins of the horses of those who had dismounted. Another five riders sat their horses, watching and talking.

These were no exotic Europeans with titles. They were homegrown native-born Americans. They wore no hoods, masks, or robes. They were dressed in ordinary civilian clothes. Their voices held no foreign accents, but instead had the flat twangy tones of the Westerner. They looked like ordinary citizens—ranchers, townsmen, laborers. They looked like a lot of posses that had chased Slocum in the past.

He raised up with the rifle and started shooting. The four in the graveyard were almost on him, at point-blank range. They looked scared out of their wits when they suddenly saw him pop out of the grave with a shouldered rifle.

He worked the lever, cranking out bullets. Three died where they stood. The fourth managed to take a few lurching steps to one side before he was cut down.

The bodies tumbled to the ground. One of the two men standing on the slope managed to throw himself facedown, out of the line of fire. The other wasn't so lucky. He was dodging when Slocum's bullet tagged him high on the shoulder, spinning him around before he flopped out of sight.

The five mounted men had their guns out and were firing, wheeling their wild-eyed horses, showering the graveyard with lead. The firepower was so heavy that Slocum had to duck down and take cover.

Crosses came apart in a shower of wooden splinters and

shards. The wrought-iron crosses rang like chimes when they were tagged. Bullets plowed into the earth or ricocheted off stones.

The firepower was getting mighty hot. Shots came from different directions as the riders fanned out around the knoll, pumping lead in Slocum's general direction.

They were moving to surround him. He regretted not having the gun that he had planted in Manfred's hand. It would have proved useful for close work when they rushed him. He craned his head, peeking over the top of the grave as much as he dared, looking for the gun.

He saw it. It was still in Manfred's hand, too far away to be reached, even if he used the rifle barrel to try to fish it closer.

Shots came from the right, the left, spraying clods of dirt into the grave, showering him.

Footsteps pounded from the east. It was the man who had ducked for cover on the slope. Now he charged, firing a six-gun. Slocum shot him, and he fell a few paces short of the grave.

More gunfire crackled, new music from different guns coming from the west. Gunfire and pounding hooves. Those attacking the knoll shouted in fear and dismay as they turned their mounts to meet the new threat.

Nobody was shooting at Slocum anymore, though the exchange of gunfire was hotter and more blistering than ever. Slocum risked a peek, raising his head.

Bigelow, Aldo, and Jardeen were making a mounted charge, bearing down on what remained of the baron's men. The three were deadly pistol fighters, and they made short work of the opposition, shooting them off their horses.

Two of the five riders survived the initial fusillade. They wheeled their horses and put the spurs to them, trying to escape. Slocum shot one out of the saddle. Jardeen turned his horse and took off after the second man, riding down.

Gun smoke puffed out of his pistol barrel as he fired. His quarry reeled, almost falling off his horse. Jardeen fired again, and the man fell sideways, hitting the turf. The horse put its head down and kept on running.

The man was not dead, but wounded. He got on his hands and knees and started crawling. Jardeen reined to a halt nearby, pulling so hard on the bit that his horse reared, rising up on its hind legs. Jardeen fired down into the wounded man. The man fell flat before the horse's forelegs touched ground.

Slocum hoisted himself out of the grave, brushing the dirt off his clothes. He took his gun from Manfred's dead hand and dropped it into his holster.

He touched hand to forehead, saluting the fallen soldier. "Thanks, Captain—and adios."

On the south side of the knoll, Bigelow sat his horse. He swung out the cylinder of his gun, shucking the empty brass into the dirt and reloading.

Bigelow said, "Looks like we saved your bacon, Slocum."

"You saved your own, Dan."

"Huh? Whaddaya mean?"

"As you may have noticed, there's been a slight change in plans," Slocum said dryly, indicating the carnage all about with a sweeping gesture of his hand.

Jardeen and Aldo rode up, joining them. Slocum said, "Where's Primus?"

"He's back there with the horses. Here he comes now," Bigelow said.

Primus rode up, trailing the string of extra horses. Slocum said, "Took your time, didn't you?"

"I'm a dynamiter, not a gunman," Primus said. "All I'd do in a shooting scrape like that is get myself killed. And then where would you be when you need something blown up?"

Jardeen said, "Where are we now? That's what I'd like to know. I don't like this business of killing men when there's no dollar signs attached to him. It goes against the grain to use my gun for free."

"It's all in a good cause, Jardeen."

"Oh, yeah? What cause is that, Slocum?"

"Gold."

Slocum told them some of what he'd learned, not all, but enough for them to understand.

"I feel better now about killing these jaspers," Jardeen said. "That's that many less of them standing between us and the gold."

They crossed to the ruins of the village. Bodies were scattered about, those of ordinary men, women, and children mixed in with the nattily attired corpses of the baroness's cadre of bodyguards.

Bigelow said, "I don't see Wardell's body anywhere. Or the Turk's."

"Or Lorelei's either," said Slocum.

"Who's that, the redhead with the big tits? Why kill her? That would be a waste of prime womanflesh."

"I don't think Zoloff's crowd worries much about things like that, or they wouldn't have wiped out the whole village."

Jardeen shrugged. "Dead men tell no tales."

"Or maybe they just like killing," Slocum said.

"Doesn't everybody?"

18

Nikolai Zoloff said, "You are about to see something which has not been seen in this hemisphere for over a hundred and fifty years. The public burning of a heretic and witch.

"That they are incarnated in one and the same person, to wit, my wayward wife Mala, only deepens the pleasure."

"I guess you never heard of the Salem witch burnings," Wardell said.

"On the contrary, my young friend, it is you who is confused about your nation's history. The witches of Salem were hanged, not burned, by the Pilgrim fathers."

Wardell shrugged. "So what? It's all pretty much the same thing, isn't it, Baron?"

"Not at all. Such matters demand fine discriminations. As a prospective member of our Order, you must pay close attention to the history of our illustrious past."

"I respect that past, but I'm more interested in your glorious future."

"You are forward-thinking, like most of your countrymen. Having no past, Americans care only about the future. It is different for such as I. And yet, who knows?

"Perhaps the Order has allowed itself to fall behind the times, here in our splendid isolation from the rest of the world. What we need is new ideas, new blood. Only that way may we surpass old glories with future triumphs.

"That is why I have reached out to recruit select outsiders such as yourself, Arlen, hard men who share our Order's age-old traditions of blood, gold, and power."

"Baron, with the application of some American business know-how, which I've got in spades, and with today's lethal firepower, you and your Order can carve out your own private empire in the Southwest and beyond!"

"May it be so, my friend, may it be so. A worthy sentiment, and one worth toasting with some more of this fine Napoleon brandy."

Lorelei said, "It would be wise not to celebrate until the baroness—and Slocum and his men—are dead."

The three were in a luxurious apartment on the ground floor of a wing of the mission church of Santa Sangre. The structure was attached to, but separate from, the church proper, and was used to house administrative offices and private living quarters for high-ranking officials of the Order.

The big room had whitewashed stucco walls, a dark tile floor, and plenty of finely polished woodwork. The massive stone fireplace was big enough for a man to stand inside without having to bend his head. There was no fire now, during the hot months.

The walls were hung with antique shields, coats of arms, and the crossed swords of conquistadors and crusaders. A pair of man-sized suits of armor, complete from head to toe, stood mounted upright on a pair of pedestals, flanking the door.

There was a writing desk as big as a billiards table, and straight-backed thronelike chairs with cordovan leather cushions. Light was provided by ornate wrought-iron candelabras with many slim waxy tapers lit to give the room a rich yellow-amber glow.

Zoloff came out from behind the desk. He was a heavy-set, fastidiously groomed man. His crest of thick black hair was gray at the temples, with not a hair out of place. His eyebrows came to points in the middle. His baggy brown eyes were like moist stones set in puffy leather pouches. He had a neatly trimmed mustache and goatee. His elegant black jacket was carefully tailored to minimize a comfortable paunch. He was thick in the torso and hips, with slim legs and small, narrow feet. He was unarmed—a weapon would have flawed the lines of his clothes.

He crossed to the sideboard, where Wardell stood waiting, empty brandy snifter in hand. Wardell was dressed more or less the same way he usually was, but he had on a suit of fresh clean clothes and his boots were newly polished.

Lorelei stood off to one side, frowning. She wore a tight, low-cut, sleeveless green silk dress, and pale green ankle boots with high heels and pointed toes.

Zoloff reached for the brandy, refilling Wardell's glass. "Come join us, Lorelei, dear."

She went to them, the folds of her dress rustling as she moved. Zoloff poured some brandy in a glass and handed it to her.

"Don't pout, darling. It makes wrinkles," he said.

Lorelei said, "Slocum worries me."

Wardell said, "Are you worried about him, or for him?"

"The man means nothing to me, nothing."

"You slept with him."

"I slept with you too, and that also meant nothing."

Wardell flushed, the veins in his neck and head swelling. Before he could reply, Zoloff broke in.

"Tut-tut," he said, "it's unseemly for us to be quarreling amongst ourselves, particularly at this auspicious moment."

He purred with pleasure. He actually liked to see his associates quarreling, since that made it more unlikely that they would form a combination against him. It was the old story of "divide and rule."

He said airily, "This man Slocum, what is he? A gunman for hire, a peasant. A minor irritant that will soon be eliminated."

"Do not underestimate him, Baron," said Lorelei. "You have not met the man. I have."

"I'll say," Wardell said sourly.

"He's cunning and ruthless, and they say he's like lightning on the draw."

"No one can outdraw a bullet in the back, my dear Lorelei. And that's what he and his men are going to get when they ride into Three Forks tomorrow.

"If a wily old fox like Captain Manfred fell into the trap, with his cadre of trained men, what chance have this pretty American desperado and his gang of brigands got? They won't escape, I assure you," Zoloff said.

"All the same, I'll rest easier when I know he's dead," said Lorelei.

"By tomorrow at this time, you'll see his body—and that of his friends—on display outside in the courtyard."

Wardell said, "I'll drink to that. I'm only sorry I won't have the opportunity to kill him myself."

Lorelei snickered. "I'd like to see you try."

"Think I can't take him?" Wardell patted the holstered gun on his hip. "I'm pretty damned fast on the draw myself."

"Don't worry, Arlen," Zoloff said. "You'll have plenty of opportunities to use your gun soon in the days ahead, as the Order begins its plan of conquest in the outside world. Terror will be the order of the day: the knife in the back, the bullet in the brain, the assassins who may strike at any hour of the day or night.

"For now, the Order is small in numbers but fanatical in determination. At first, we will have to strike in secret, creating a shadow reign of terror, slaying a lawman here, a legislator there, until these peasants learn that to defy us means sudden death when it's least expected.

"Later, when our ranks have been swelled by fresh recruits, we will be able to operate more openly, with roving bands of mounted guerrillas ready to sweep out of the mountains and spread death to the cities of the plains," Zoloff declared.

Wardell nodded. "You'll be the most powerful man in the Southwest, Baron."

" 'Tis a consummation devoutly to be wished, and one worth drinking to. And so, my friends, if you will join me . . ."

Zoloff raised his brandy glass. Lorelei and Wardell moved in, raising their glasses to his. He said, "Through the Order of Santa Sangre, to blood, gold, and power!"

They clinked glasses and drank. Lorelei tossed hers back in one fierce gulp. Zoloff said, "This brandy was set up in casks when Napoleon was emperor of most of Europe. It's extremely rare and meant to be savored a sip at a time, dear lady."

"Bah! I hope it is luckier for us than it was for him," Lorelei said.

"She's so impetuous," Zoloff said, chuckling. "That's why she couldn't bear to be a lady-in-waiting to my dear wife. My soon-to-be-late-and-unlamented wife."

Wardell said, "That reminds me, Baron, won't the ceremony be happening soon?"

"Indeed it will, my friend."

"Don't we have to get ready?"

"A small matter of donning our robes and going down to the church courtyard when the others have assembled. We still have a bit of time left, I believe.

"Still, it would be good to check on the progress of the procession. After all, I wouldn't want to be late to my own wife's burning!"

Glass in hand, Zoloff crossed to a set of French doors opposite the door to the room. He turned the latch, opening the doors on a outdoor patio that overlooked the sprawling church courtyard.

The mission complex was set on a flat-topped rise. A gentle slope led down to the town of Frater an eighth of a mile below. The town was a little smaller in size and population than Los Palos.

Now, on this night, the town was dark. Not a soul ventured forth on its empty streets; not a light burned in any window. It might have been a city of the dead. The vast majority of the population, very much alive, huddled in their dark houses behind locked doors and shuttered windows, hoping that nobody came for them.

A sliver of a horned moon hung high in the eastern sky, which was clear of all but a few tattered wisps of cloud. The stars were bright but remote. Moonlight shone on roofs, chimneys, and paving stones, and on the peaks of jagged mountains encircling the valley.

Nearer, in the church courtyard, there stood an upright eight-foot-tall pillar, a stake surrounded by heaping mounds of firewood.

Zoloff looked out on the scene. "Over a quarter century ago, I came to America to join Emperor Maximilian in his attempt to hold the throne of Mexico for the Austrian empire. We Hyundagari were vassals of the Austrians, and were required to levy troops to send overseas to fight the forces of the revolutionist Juarez.

"Maximilian lost his crown, his queen, and his life in front of a firing squad. Those of us who were left had to survive as best we could. It was then that I learned of the Holy Order of Santa Sangre, from a few of the brotherhood who had journeyed south to fight against the godless Juaristas. When they fled north, I escaped with them here, to this place. And so I became an iniate in the Order, and rose through the ranks as the years passed.

"I kept in contact with my ancestral homeland across the sea, and when an Austro-Hungarian imperial intrigue seized the principality, I offered my protection to the royal Hyundagarian refugees, among whom was Mala Valerian, the soon-to-be ex-baroness. And so I acquired a bride, a title, and a patent of nobility.

"And now, after long struggles, I am the Master of the Order, while Mala will soon be nothing more than a handful of cinders, ashes, and charred bones—and an unpleasant memory!

"My only regret is that I have no sons to share this triumph with me. But there will be other women, other brides, many of them—and many sons. So do I swear!"

Zoloff drained his glass, then hurled it down into the courtyard, where it shattered against the stones.

At that moment, an iron bell in the mission belfrey began to toll, striking low, ponderous, sinister echoes across the valley.

Zoloff turned, facing Lorelei and Wardell. There was high color in his face and his eyes glittered.

He said, "The bell calls the brotherhood to assemble. Now the final act begins!"

19

The bell tolled thirteen times. As the last mournful echoes died away, torches were lit in the plaza of Frater. One, two, many flames sprang up, until there were at least forty of them being borne by the robed, hooded procession.

The Knights of the Order of Santa Sange had filtered through the empty streets and lanes of the town, in groups of twos and threes, obedient to the summoning of the bell, massing in the central square.

The townsfolk who were not of the order cowered in their homes, praying that they would live to see the dawn. Sometimes, for no particular reason known outside the Order, the knights would fall without warning on some individual or entire family, carrying them off to never be seen again. The citizens didn't dare to steal a peek at the procession, for it was death for "profane" eyes to gaze upon the doings of the Order.

This night, though, there were some particularly profane eyes out and about in the streets.

The members of the Order were outfitted in dark monk's robes with peaked hoods, shadowing their faces. Sewn over the left breast of each robe was the coat of arms of the secret society. The robes were cinched around the waist with thick knotted rope belts. Beneath the robes' ankle-length hems could be seen the pants and boots of today, the late 19th century.

The assembled formed up into a long column numbering ten ranks with four in each rank. At the point, a hooded giant walked alone, a few paces ahead of the rest, carrying aloft an eight-foot-tall standard topped by a golden double-headed battle-ax in the rough shape of a cross.

Among the torchbearers was a trio of drummers, each toting a brass kettle-type drum held in place by carrying-slings. With mallets in hand, they beat out a steady, monotonous, ominous rhythm that set the slow deliberate pace of the march.

The column filtered out through the west end of the plaza, starting up the slope toward the mission church, rearing like some forgotten fortress on top of the rise.

In the center of the line of march was a donkey bearing the condemned prisoner, the baroness. In accordance with the ritual, she sat backward on the mount, outfitted in the garments of humiliation: a long white pointed cap oddly similar to the dunce's cap for backward pupils, and a simple white shift decorated with a six-pointed Seal of Solomon, a crescent moon, and other astrological signs and symbols associated with heresy and black magic.

Her hands were tied behind her back, and a rope halter with a hangman's noose circled her neck. Her back was straight and her chin was held high.

The weird procession passed through a lane between two rows of two-story houses, the drumming and hollow-voiced chanting of the cultists echoing off the walls.

All but the tail end of the procession had now broken out on to the open slope. The last four men in line held slightly back from the others as they brought up the rear.

Each member of the foursome held his torch high, so

none of its light could reveal the faces hid within heavily shadowed cowls. It might also be observed that their chanting was not up to standard, and that they had a tendency to mumble, hum, and otherwise fake it. But the racket of the drum beating and the deep, swelling chants of the main body of the column drowned out mistakes that might have been otherwise noticed by suspicious ears.

Furthermore, under the folds of their baggy robes, the figures of the quartet bulked larger than life-sized, and had a tendency to clank and rattle, as if weighed down with masses of hardware.

But the rest of the column was looking forward, not behind, except for the baroness, and she was too deeply involved in her own bitter thoughts to take notice of such things.

Like a snake whose scales were fire, the torch-bearing procession climbed the shallow slope, entering the church courtyard. Firelight, smoke, and shadows created a scene of lurid unreality.

In the room overlooking the courtyard, Nikolai Zoloff donned a robe over his garments. Unlike those of the rank-and-file members massing in the courtyard, this robe was made of black silk with a scarlet lining, and was decorated with intricately embroidered crests and heralds of the Order.

"It's time for us to join the others," Zoloff said. "Put on your robe and we'll go down into the courtyard, Wardell."

Wardell put on a white hooded robe. "I feel like a damned fool in this getup."

"The white robe is traditional for when a new member is initiated into the Order. These ritual observances are highly important to such an ancient group as ours. They provide continuity over the centuries, and help protect the brotherhood against the blandishments of the modern world.

"Ours is an ultra-conservative organization in many ways, Arlen. Why, we have yet to officially recognize the Copernican doctrine that the Earth revolves around the sun!

"But such attitudes can be dangerous in a world of Maxim guns and ironclad warships. That is why I have reached out to those like yourself, to help us keep pace with changing times," Zoloff said.

He crossed to Wardell and made a few minor adjustments on the white robe, so that it fit properly.

"There, that's better! Now you are properly attired to be welcomed into our ranks. And now we must take our place with the others," Zoloff said.

He turned to Lorelei. "I regret that your sex prohibits you from joining us, my dear, but you'll have an excellent view of the burning from here."

"I am only sorry that I cannot watch from close up, to see the baroness burn. It is a sight I have been anticipating for some considerable time," said Lorelei.

Zoloff went to the open French doors, standing framed in the doorway as he looked out on the courtyard, which was now filled with chanting black-clad cultists.

"It appears that the baroness has just made her entrance," he said.

Wardell joined him, looking over his shoulder. "Why the dunce cap and the donkey?"

"Ah, that goes to the very heart of the matter! You will be privileged to witness a modern-day version of the auto-da-fé, the 'act of faith,' as the burning of witches and heretics is traditionally called. This is the time-honored ritual prescribed by the Holy Office of the Inquisition. The one who is to be burned is first publicly mocked and humiliated with the cap and the dress and by being paraded riding backward on an ass. The point being that first the sinner's pride is destroyed, and then the sinner—thus, the Devil—is mocked.

"A quaint and charming bit of historical pageantry that few outside the Order will ever see," Zoloff added. He raised the hood of his robe, fitting it over his head, motioning for Wardell to do the same.

"And now, on to the festivities," he said. He stepped out on to the courtyard, Wardell following.

Lorelei stood in the doorway, clawlike hands clutching the door frame, her face feral and avid for destruction.

Down in the courtyard, the cultists were massed around the stake. A stir went through their hooded ranks when they saw the Master of the Order appear on the patio, accompanied by the white-robed initiate. They knew that the burning was about to begin.

In the rear of the mass, near the edge of the courtyard, there was another kind of burning, as one of the last men in line lit the end of a thick fat cigar on a torch, put it between his lips, and began puffing it.

The profane and worldly scent of cigar smoke wafted forward, drifting among the rear ranks of the cultists. A couple of them turned their heads, looking sharply behind them to see who was guilty of this act of near-blasphemy.

The cigar was clamped between the jaws of a hooded man. He drew on the cigar, causing the orange dot at its end to flare brighter, revealing his face.

It was Slocum. He brought a hand out from within the folds of his robe, clutching a bundle of dynamite with a very short fuse. He touched the lit end of the cigar to that fuse, which began fizzing like a Fourth of July sparkler.

He tossed the lit bundle into the middle of the cultists.

The explosion sent cloaked bodies flying headfirst into the air as if they had been launched by catapults.

He and his three partners shucked off their robes for better freedom of movement. They were walking arsenals, armed to the teeth. Slocum wore a canvas bag down at his side, held in place by a cross-chest shoulder sling. The pouch was filled with bundles of dynamite like the one he had just thrown.

He lit another one and threw it, sending more blasted bodies and body parts into the air.

Bigelow unlimbered the shotgun that he'd been carrying under his robe, cutting loose with both barrels into the cultists at point-blank range.

A pair of six-guns leaped into the long-fingered ghostly white hands of Jardeen, blazing away. He fired one shot from the gun in his right, one from the left, then one from the right, alternating between the guns, shooting so fast that the reports sounded like those of a Gatling gun. Each shot hit its target, and each target was a member of the Order.

Aldo was there, holding a Winchester leveled at waist height, working the lever to crank out rounds into the fast-dwindling ranks of the enemy.

After the first dynamite blast, the baroness had fallen off the back of the jackass, which made a blind panicked run in the opposite direction. The woman fell on her side on the flags of the courtyard, lying flat—the best place to be once the shooting started.

Slocum had tossed the dynamite bundles as far away from the baroness as possible, yet where they would still inflict maximum casualties on the cultists. By necessity he had thrown the explosives up toward the front of the group, so the back-blast wouldn't tag him and his men.

The three gunmen, Bigelow, Jardeen, and Aldo, mowed down the nearer ranks in a blistering onslaught of firepower.

This was no gunfight, it was slaughter! The cultists never knew what hit them. Those not cut down in the initial fusillade broke and ran, shrieking, scattering.

Now that the enemy's ranks were no longer massed together, the dynamite was less effective. Slocum shucked off the carrying pouch and laid it down on the stones— gently.

He and the other three moved away from it. Some of the cultists who had fled the initial destruction were now massing on the sidelines, firing back. Slocum and company didn't want to be in the vicinity of that sack of dynamite if a stray slug should hit it.

The courtyard was filled with gunsmoke, blood, and bodies. Slocum and his friends had the advantage—anybody standing in their way was an enemy and therefore fair game, while the cultists had to worry about accidentally shooting their own men.

The choking smoke made it hard to see. Slocum made his way toward where he'd last seen the baroness. Some black-clad figures loomed out of the smoke, blocking his way. Gunfire cut them down.

Slocum almost tripped over a white-clad body sprawled at his feet: the baroness. He dropped to one knee beside her, fearing for an awful instant that she was dead—and then how would he get the gold?

But she wasn't dead, or even shot; she was just playing possum while the battle raged. He gripped her smooth white shoulder and turned her so he could see her face. It was bruised, wide-eyed, taut with strain, but still beautiful.

"Evening, Baroness."

"You!"

"Sure, who'd you expect? When I make a date with a lady, I always keep it. You all right?"

"Yes—yes!"

"Where's the gold?"

"Get me out of here and I'll take you to it!"

"Sure thing."

Small firefights had broken out in the courtyard. Each gun had its own music. There was the big bass booming of Bigelow's double-barreled shotgun, the high-powered report of Aldo's Winchester, and the almost mechanical *pop-pop-popping* of Jardeen's Colts. Each time the scattered handfuls of cultists tried to rally a counterattack, they would be drowned out and silenced by the blasting of the three gunfighters.

The baroness said, "Can you untie my hands?"

"Just as soon as I reload." Slocum swung out the cyclinder of his gun, spilling the spent brass on courtyard stones.

A nightmare figure loomed up out of the gray-white gunsmoke, charging. Its hood was thrown back, revealing the shaved skull and fiercely glowering face of the Turk.

He carried the cultic standard in both hands, using it as a lance. The upper half was made of the gold double-headed battle-ax, while the lower half was a stout wooden shaft. Between the twin blades of the ax was a foot-long spike, like a needle-sharp pike blade.

His target was not Slocum, but the baroness. With her dead, the secret of the treasure would be safe in the sole possession of Zoloff.

Slocum let the empty gun fall from his hand as he rose up to meet the Turk's lunge. There wasn't even time for him to draw his knife. The Turk was thrusting downward, intending to run the baroness through and spear her to the pavement.

Slocum leaped forward, meeting the Turk's charge. He stepped inside the angle of the thrusting spear, slamming a shoulder into the Turk's midsection, while at the same time batting the pole down and to the side.

It was like butting into a charging bull. The Turk was a half a head taller than Slocum, and outweighed him by some fifty-odd pounds. But Slocum managed to break up his timing.

The golden spike struck the pavement six inches from

the baroness, then skittered to one side as Slocum pushed it outward. He was unable to break the other's grip, and clung to the wooden spear shaft as the Turk's charge knocked him off balance.

Slocum slammed an elbow into the Turk's middle—it was like hitting a tree trunk. The Turk went "Whump!" but that was about all. Slocum back-fisted him in the face, splattering his nose into pulp. That hurt, and the Turk roared.

Slocum fell sideways across the shaft, breaking it in half. He fell to the pavement, tucking his arms close to his sides and thus absorbing the impact of a brutal kick that would otherwise have smashed his ribs.

The Turk held about four feet of wooden shaft, and was winding up to drive the jagged broken end into Slocum, spearing him. Twisting on the ground, Slocum swung the battle-ax in a vicious circular thrust that caught the Turk above the ankle.

Blood spurted as the razor-sharp blade bit deep into flesh and bone. His footing cut out from under him, the Turk collapsed.

Slocum got his feet under him and rose, clutching the haft of the battle-ax in both hands. The Turk lay on his back, trying to rise up. He raised his hands as if to stop the descent of the glittering ax, which Slocum raised and then brought down in a vicious golden arc.

The ax blade rang out against the pavement, having chopped through the Turk's neck, sending his head bounding across the flagstones.

Slocum slipped on blood, narrowly avoiding a slug that whipped past his head like an angry bumblebee, ricocheting off the pavement.

The shot came from Wardell, standing on the patio with rifle in hand, swinging it around for a second shot.

But Aldo had seen him and was already in action, point-

ing the Winchester at him, firing. The slug caught Wardell
in the middle, causing him to jerk the rifle up as he stumbled back, firing into the sky.

Aldo sent another slug into him, and another. Wardell
staggered, reeling, as the blood from three holes in his middle came gushing to soak the front of his white robe.

He fell backward, dead.

The surviving cultists had fled. Slocum used the ax blade
to saw through the cruel ropes binding the baroness's
hands. She rubbed and chafed her wrists, trying to restore
circulation.

"Bring the ax," she said. "You'll need it to get the
gold."

Slocum hurriedly reloaded his gun. He gripped the baroness by the arm, helping her to her feet. She leaned against
him for support. Through the thin shift he could feel the
warmth of her body. Her hair smelled sweet.

Shots rang out. A wounded cultist caught Aldo by surprise, shooting him down. Slocum put a bullet in the
shooter's head.

He looked around. The burning stake lay on its side,
knocked over by one of the dynamite blasts. Black-clad
bodies painted with red blood littered the courtyard. The
gun smoke had mostly cleared, though some ghostly
streamers of it hung drifting over the stones like phantom
wraiths.

The surviving cultists had fled. Slocum, Jardeen, and the
baroness were still standing. Aldo was dead and Bigelow
was down, mortally wounded.

20

"Just keep me alive long enough to see that beautiful gold, that's all I ask."

"Hell, you'll live long enough to spend it, Dan."

"Don't bullshit a bullshitter, Slocum. I ain't gonna live long with a bullet in the guts, so get to it."

Their voices had a hollow, echoing quality, caused by the vast, high-ceilinged space of the interior of the old mission church. It was ornate and baroque, with huge square-sided pillars, vaulted pointed arches, and intricate decorations.

They were at the far end of the space, at the foot of a massive altar. The light was provided by torches that had been placed around the immediate area, filling it with a zone of radiance. Beyond the altar, the vaulted precincts of the structure were mysterious and gloomy.

At the opposite end of the nave, which spanned the long axis of the church, the east-facing front double-doors were flung open on the nighted landscape.

Outside, Primus stood watch, ready to give the alarm at the first sign of trouble. During the battle earlier, he'd been safely hidden away, watching the train of horses that would be needed for the getaway.

Standing at the foot of the altar were Slocum, Jardeen, and the baroness. Nearby, sitting slumped with his back against a pillar, was Bigelow. A priceless antique tapestry had been torn into strips and used to wrap his middle. He'd caught a bullet in the belly during the battle, and the wrappings were meant to keep his life from leaking out too soon. He was pale as marble.

Slocum said, "Keep an eye peeled for Zoloff and the others. We didn't kill them all off, so they might be back."

The baroness nodded. "Nikolai will be back, be sure of it. He's not one to give up while the breath remains in his body."

Jardeen said, "I'm keeping my eyes peeled for that gold. Where is it?"

Slocum said, "Baroness?"

"Come . . . and bring the ax." She crossed to one side of the altar, where a monumental statue stood on a black stone pedestal the size of a foundation cornerstone. The statue was of a man holding a sword aloft. On the base of the pedestal was a tarnished brass plaque identifying the statue as St. James—in Spanish Iago—Santiago, the patron saint of the New World conquistadors.

"Pry off the plaque," the baroness said.

The battle-ax was not made of gold, but only gold-plated. Beneath the gilt, the double-headed blade and spike were made of solid steel.

Slocum wedged the blade under the edge of the plaque and pried it off. It came loose with a deep metallic groan, like an iron saint moaning.

Beneath the plaque, set in the center of the face of the pedestal block, was a long vertical slot.

The baroness said, "That is the keyhole, the ax is the key."

Slocum held the ax so its head was at right angles to the floor. He fitted it spike-first into the slot. When the ax head was fully inserted, so that only the haft was showing, there was a hollow metallic click.

Slocum turned the haft clockwise. There was an initial resistance. Then the interior tumblers turned, with a dull mechanical *thunk*, like a heavy spring being tripped.

The resistance vanished, and the ax turned freely inside. A half-inch gap showed at the top of the block face, an inch or two below the upper edge.

The pedestal was hollow, and the front face was an outward-opening hinged lid. Slocum removed the ax and lowered the face outward and down, until it lay flat on the floor.

Inside the pedestal was an ancient ironbound chest, made of oak aged so that it was almost black. Its short end faced him. There was a handle, and he took hold of it and pulled the chest out. It was heavy, and he had to use some muscle to haul it into the light.

Jardeen and the baroness clustered around him while Slocum used his knife to pry open the lid of the chest, which was sealed with age and corrosion. It came loose suddenly, falling back and tearing loose from its rotted leather hinges.

Light blossomed under the altar, as torchlight reflected on the mass of gold and jewels heaped to the brim of the treasure chest, filling the scene with a golden glow.

"Let me see, dammit," Bigelow said.

Slocum went to him. Bigelow held a gun in his lap. Slocum said, "What's that for?"

"I was figuring Jardeen for a double cross while everybody was watching the gold," Bigelow said.

Jardeen said, "Sorry to disappoint you, Dan."

"You must be getting reformed, Jardeen."

"Why not? I can afford scruples now that I'm a rich man."

Bigelow choked back a groan as Slocum helped him up. Slocum hesitated. Bigelow spoke through clenched teeth: "C'mon, c'mon. I don't have much time left, so don't stall now."

Slocum got one of Bigelow's arms across his shoulders and half walked, half carried him to the treasure trove.

"We sure showed 'em something, huh, Slocum?"

"You bet, Dan. They'll be telling this story a hundred years from now."

"Not bad for a fat old man . . ."

Bigelow's face was underlit by the golden glow as he stood hunched over the chestful of glittering plunder.

"Beautiful! Beautiful," he said, dying.

Then he was deadweight in Slocum's arms, and Slocum had to ease him down to the floor.

21

Dawn was breaking as the raiders prepared to leave Santa Sangre. The gold treasure was in sacks that had been loaded on to the packhorses. Slocum, Jardeen, and the baroness were on horseback, ready to ride out.

They were a fair distance away from the mission. Doc Primus squatted outside the front entrance of the church, preparing the final salute.

Down the hill, the town of Frater was still locked up tight, none of its citizens having yet dared to emerge into the dawn of a new day to see what the previous night's carnage had wrought.

Primus took one last look into the church's gloomy interior. At the far end, stretched out on their backs below the altar, lay the bodies of Bigelow and Aldo, each holding a silent gun in his hand.

Throughout the church, fastened to the key load-bearing pillars that supported the structure's enormous weight, were bundles of dynamite, each linked to a master fuse, the end of which lay curling at the feet of Doc Primus as he knelt over it, lit match in hand.

He looked up, glancing across the way at the others.

Slocum gave him the signal, bringing an arm down in a chopping motion. Primus lit the fuse, waited until he was sure that it was going well and good, and then ran like hell.

He had cut a long length of fuse cord, but even so, he ran away as fast as his stubby little legs could carry him.

He had just reached the others, a safe distance away, when the blast blew. The mission church exploded like a volcano blowing its top, then collapsed in a mound of smoking rubble.

When the last booming echo of the blast had died away, Slocum said, "If the Order ever starts up again, they'll find Aldo and Bigelow's ghosts waiting for them."

"Amen," said Primus.

22

Not all of the Order had been wiped out at the big gunfight at the mission. Some had managed to flee the bullets and bombs of Slocum's raiders. Also, not all the members had been present at the ceremony-turned-slaughter. Some were out on the roving patrols that routinely ranged over the valley and its environs, searching for interlopers and travelers who would be easy prey.

By mid-morning, the stunned cultists had managed to muster close to two dozen men, who mounted up and gave chase to Slocum and company. Slocum's band had a couple of hours' head start, but was slowed by the golden treasure weighing down the packhorses, and the need to reserve some strength and energy in their animals for the long haul through mountains and desert.

Their pursuers were not encumbered. Their only goal was to destroy the raiders and recapture the gold, and whether they killed their horses by riding them to the death in breakneck pursuit meant nothing at all to them.

Last night, they had been taken by surprise, outgunned and massacred—their own usual mode of operation, but one they were as helpless to resist as their victims had been in the past. But those who had been out on patrol, and returned to their home to find their fellows dead, their shrine leveled, and their treasure gone, were consumed with a white-hot rage.

They overtook the raiders in late afternoon, coming in sight of them as they rode through the Three Forks valley.

The pursuers were riding hard and raising plenty of dust, which could be seen a long way off. The time for holding back was done, as Slocum and company put the spurs to their horses.

The raiders made a wide swing west around the ruined village, which had become a feasting ground for flocks of buzzards that had gathered by the score to feast on the bodies strewn about the site. The village square and the graveyard on the knoll looked like the setting for a vultures' convention. The big birds were on the ground, clustered in numbers so great that they hid the bodies on which they fed. Most of the bodies had long since been picked clean, but the carrion-eaters squawked and jostled for every last little scrap remaining on the bones.

Slocum's band made their way not toward the eastern wall gap, but rather toward the mouth of the winding westward canyon. Slocum had reckoned from the start on a possible pursuit, which had led to his strategy of using the old mining site as a base for his approach from the west.

The knights of the Order opened fire as soon as they saw Slocum's group's dust. They were too far away to hit anything, but it made them feel better. Their horses were already in a lather from the long hard ride, and now the hunters whipped and spurred them mercilessly, seeing the kill near at hand.

Slocum's band rode into the westward canyon, their pursuers now only a few hundred yards behind. Riding in single file, the raiders and the gold-laden horses plunged at breakneck speed into the twists and turns of the rocky gorge.

Canyon walls narrowed, until the trail became so thin that a rider extending both arms out straight from the shoulders could graze both walls with the fingertips.

While the others raced on ahead, Slocum and Doc Primus stayed behind. Slocum shucked a Winchester out of the saddle scabbard as he hopped down to the ground. He held the reins of both horses as Primus busied himself at a pre-selected spot at the side of the trail.

Earlier, when first coming through the gorge toward Three Forks, Slocum had had Primus mine the site. Clumps of dynamite were placed at key spots going up the walls of the canyons on both sides.

Now, from further back along the trail, came the sound of gunfire and approaching riders. The gorge echoed the din, making it sound like rolling thunder racing west toward Slocum and Primus. Bullets spanged off the rocks, leaving lead smears and whining ricochets.

Slocum stood to one side of his horse, resting his rifle across the saddle, holding both sets of reins in his free hand.

The point man of the riders came into view, galloping hellbent for leather. Slocum shot not him, but his horse. The horse collapsed, throwing the rider headlong and blocking the trail.

The rider was dazed but still moving, so Slocum shot him too. "Hurry up, Doc!"

Primus jumped up, dashing away from the now-lit and sputtering fuse, shouting the traditional cry of the dynamiter when a live explosive is about to blow:

"Fire in the hole!"

More pursuers were knotted up behind the fallen horse and rider. Slocum threw more lead at them, while Primus gathered up the reins of his animal and threw himself into the saddle with an agility that was well-nigh astonishing for one so sedentary as himself.

He turned the horse's head west, put spurs to flank, and took off like lightning down the gorge.

The sizzling fuse cord consumed itself as it followed a burning line up the side of the ravine, toward the planted clumps of dynamite.

Slocum swung up into the saddle and took off, chased by bullets that buzzed around him like a swarm of maddened wasps. A passing slug lifted the corner of his vest, while a ricochet sprayed his face with tiny rock chips.

Then came the blast as the dynamite blew, bringing down hundreds of tons of rocks down on the Order's riders.

Smoke, heat, and pressure waves raced along the gorge, barely missing Slocum as he rounded a blind corner and was protected from the force of the blast.

When the dust cleared, the canyon was blocked by giant stone slabs heaped twenty feet high. Beneath them lay the cultists.

Slocum found Primus waiting for him a little further up the trail. Slocum said, "Now I know why I keep you around, Doc."

"Am I good or am I good?"

"You're a firecracker. Let's ride. I don't want the others to get too far ahead of us. Might give them ideas."

23

Daylight was closing fast when Slocum and company finally broke out of the westward gorge to the old mining site. Gloom lay thick on the oval flat, and the only light in the sky was a vivid yellow-red razor-line in the west.

Primus said, "Let's dig up the water cans and supplies fast, before the bats come out."

"Scared of a few bats, Doc?" Slocum said.

"Yes!"

"Stay out of their way and they won't bother you, which is more than you can say for some people."

Jardeen said, "How true." He stood facing Slocum, pulling his gloves off, exposing those lily-white hands.

"So it's come to this, eh, Jardeen?"

"We've got some unfinished business, Slocum."

"That suits me fine."

The baroness stared in astonishment. "Are you men mad? A fortune in gold, and all you can think of is fighting?"

"Not all, ma'am," Jardeen said mockingly. "As soon as I've gotten rid of him, I aim to get much better acquainted with you."

" 'Fraid not, Jardeen. You'll be keeping a date with the worms," said Slocum.

Primus took the baroness by the arm and moved her back, out of the line of fire.

"Almighty sure of yourself, eh, Slocum?"

"That's right, Jardeen."

"One thing you didn't figure on, tall man. You're covered. Dennis and some of the boys have got you under their guns. You're not the only one who knows how to trap-shoot."

"All I see is you."

"Let him know you're here, nephew!"

From the rocks in front of the mine tunnel came a metallic cricketing, the sound of hammers being cocked.

"Not so funny now, is it, Slocum?"

"Bigelow had you figured right all along when he said you'd try to pull a double cross, Jardeen."

"Dan always was a pretty good judge of character. Too bad he's not here now. Dennis would've liked evening up the score for that mauling he gave him. Oh, well, I suppose he'll have to be satisfied with his share of the gold . . . and the woman, when I'm done with her.

"I confess I got a mite worried when you decided to come here first instead of Three Forks. That's where I told Dennis to be waiting, and once we were on the trail, I didn't have the chance to slip word to him about the change in plans.

"But I fixed that when we were in the graveyard. I wrote him a note telling him to wait here, then pinned it to a tree where he couldn't miss seeing it.

"Come out and say hello to the man before we kill him, Dennis. Don't be shy, nephew. Dennis? Dennis!"

Figures rose from behind the rocks. The light was almost all gone, but even in the murky shadows, there was no mistaking the identity of the man in the center of the group of five armed men.

"Nikolai!" said the baroness, gasping.

It was hard to tell who was more shocked, she or Jardeen.

Zoloff held a six-gun leveled at the raiders, while his four vigilant cultists were armed with pistols and rifles.

Zoloff said, "You'll find your nephew and the rest of his friends behind the rocks, where we left them after we killed them. You see, one of my men also found the note at Three Forks. He left it there, and was returning to Santa Sangre to tell me about it when the late unpleasantness broke out last night."

"Huh! Well, that's a horse on me," Jardeen said.

"Quite so."

From deep within the tunnel's depths came a faint flutter of motion, a subtle disturbance as much felt as heard. Slocum and Jardeen both picked up on it, but Zoloff and his gunmen were oblivious to it.

Slocum said, "How'd you get here, fly? I know you didn't come through the gorge before we did."

"Fly? Almost," Zoloff said. "On top of the mine is a plateau, a mesa top which stretches from here back to Santa Sangre. It's quite level and one can easily ride across it. Of course, there's no way to get the horses down from up there, so the way is very rarely used. We left our horses up there and climbed down—a most fatiguing climb, I assure you, and one which was relieved only by the pleasure of seeing the surprised expressions on the faces of the stupid young men who were encamped here waiting for you. It was almost as pleasant as putting an end to their stupid, useless lives.

"Needless to say, we won't be walking back. We'll take your horses, which you have so thoughtfully provided for us. And my gold."

There was a fluttering now, the sound of the beating of

many wings rising like the wind, but Zoloff was too full of himself to notice it, while his men were too well-trained to interrupt their Master while he was talking.

He said, "I can hardly fault you on the killing last night. It was most impressive. But to destroy a church which was hundreds of years old, and a rare example of Gothic-Baroque architecture in this part of the Americas, that was barbaric—unforgiveable!"

Jardeen said, "I'm only sorry we're not going to find out who's faster on the draw, Slocum, me or you."

"Don't be too sure of that."

The beating wings sounded now like a rushing river.

Zoloff said, "With the treasure recovered, the Order can start again and—*what's that?!*"

The sun's last rays now extinguished, a horde of bats erupted from the tunnel mouth in a furious, blinding whirl-wind.

Slocum and Jardeen both drew, aiming not at Zoloff and his men, but each other.

The two shots came as one, but Slocum's was a shade faster, drilling Jardeen and knocking him off balance so that when he fired at Slocum, he missed.

And then he was dead.

Zoloff and his men were square in the path of the cyclone of bats boiling out of the tunnel mouth into the night sky. The numbers were so great that the cultists couldn't see Slocum, Primus, and the baroness.

The bats weren't attacking the humans; the humans just happened to be in the way of their nightly launch skyward. Zoloff and the others stumbled around blindly, shooting into the air, beating at their heads and hair to keep the bats away, while still more hundreds and thousands of bats burst out of the tunnel.

As the last of the horde took to the sky, and Zoloff and his men were able to see again, the last thing they saw was

Slocum with a gun in each hand—his own gun and one he had taken from Jardeen's dead body.

Slocum picked them off quickly, like plinking tin ducks in a shooting gallery, and then they saw no more, ever.

A cloud lifted over the site as the bat horde flew off, scattering to the four corners of the wind. In the clear darkling sky, the evening star shone.

Primus and the baroness picked themselves up from the ground, brushing themselves off.

"Whew! Talk about 'bats out of Hell,' " Slocum said. "Or Heaven, as the case may be."

JAKE LOGAN

TODAY'S HOTTEST ACTION WESTERN!

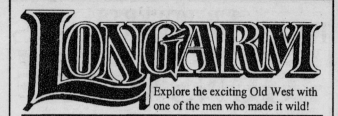